Emily Harvale lives in
– although she woul
French Alps ... or Canada ...
has several months of snow. Emily loves snow almost as much as she loves Christmas. Having worked in the City (London) for several years, Emily returned to her home town of Hastings where she spends her days writing ... and wondering if it will ever snow. You can contact her via her website, Twitter, Facebook or Instagram.
There is also a Facebook group where fans can chat with Emily about her books, her writing day and life in general. Details can be found on Emily's website.

Author contacts:
www.emilyharvale.com
www.twitter.com/emilyharvale
www.facebook.com/emilyharvalewriter
www.instagram.com/emilyharvale

***

Scan the code above to see all Emily's books on Amazon

Also by this author

The Golf Widows' Club
Sailing Solo
Carole Singer's Christmas
Christmas Wishes
A Slippery Slope
The Perfect Christmas Plan
Be Mine
It Takes Two
Bells and Bows on Mistletoe Row

Lizzie Marshall series:
Highland Fling – book 1
Lizzie Marshall's Wedding – book 2

Goldebury Bay series:
Ninety Days of Summer – book 1
Ninety Steps to Summerhill – book 2
Ninety Days to Christmas – book 3

Hideaway Down series:
A Christmas Hideaway – book 1
Catch A Falling Star – book 2
Walking on Sunshine – book 3
Dancing in the Rain – book 4

Hall's Cross series
Deck the Halls – book 1
The Starlight Ball – book 2

Michaelmas Bay series
Christmas Secrets in Snowflake Cove – book 1
Blame it on the Moonlight – book 2

Lily Pond Lane series

The Cottage on Lily Pond Lane –
Part One – New beginnings and Summer secrets
Part Two – Autumn leaves and Trick or treat
Christmas on Lily Pond Lane
Return to Lily Pond Lane
A Wedding on Lily Pond Lane
Secret Wishes and Summer Kisses on Lily Pond Lane

Wyntersleap series

Christmas at Wynter House – book 1
New Beginnings at Wynter House – book 2
A Wedding at Wynter House – book 3
Love is in the Air – spin off

Merriment Bay series

Coming Home to Merriment Bay – book 1
Chasing Moonbeams in Merriment Bay – book 2
Wedding Bells in Merriment Bay – book 3

Seahorse Harbour Novels

Summer at my Sister's – book 1
Christmas at Aunt Elsie's – book 2
Just for Christmas – book 3
Tasty Treats at Seahorse Bites Café – book 4
Dreams and Schemes at The Seahorse Inn – book 5
Weddings and Reunions in Seahorse Harbour – book 6

ISBN 978-1-909917-79-8

Published by Crescent Gate Publishing

Print edition published worldwide 2021
E-edition published worldwide 2021

Cover design by JR and Emily Harvale

Emily Harvale

Christmas at Clementine Cottage

Acknowledgements

My grateful thanks go to the following:

Christina Harkness for her patience and care in editing this book.
My webmaster, David Cleworth who does so much more than website stuff.
My cover design team, JR.
Luke Brabants. Luke is a talented artist and can be found at: www.lukebrabants.com
My wonderful friends for their friendship and love. You know I love you all.
All the fabulous members of my Readers' Club. You help and support me in so many ways and I am truly grateful for your ongoing friendship. I wouldn't be where I am today without you.
My Twitter and Facebook friends, and fans of my Facebook author page. It's great to chat with you. You help to keep me (relatively) sane!

Map of Clementine Cove

There's an interactive map, with more details, on my website: www.emilyharvale.com

To all those spending Christmas away from their loved ones.

Chapter 1

'And you're only telling me this now?'

Elodie Abbott glared at her best friend. She couldn't decide whether she was more surprised than cross, or vice-versa. She certainly wasn't happy and this news was definitely a surprise. What other secrets had Iris been hiding?

They'd been best friends since Elodie had shared a bag of salt and vinegar crisps, which she'd pinched from her elder sister, Sasha's lunchbox, with the then five-year-old Iris, and Elodie had thought that, after a friendship of more than thirty years, they knew each other inside out.

But as Elodie's gran often said, "You may think you know someone inside, outside, up, down and sideways, but you'd be surprised. People are good at keeping secrets, especially if it's something they really don't want you to know."

Iris had kept this secret well. But what Elodie couldn't fathom, was why.

Iris shrugged, and although she had the decency to look and sound a little contrite, her words belied that sentiment.

'Don't look at me like that, El. It's no biggie, is it? So I've got an uncle I haven't told you about. So what? You're not the only one who doesn't know. We never tell anyone about him. He's the black sheep of the Talbot family. *Was* the black sheep, I suppose I should say.'

'And that's supposed to make this better?' Elodie wasn't quite ready to move on from this, even though Iris was right. The existence of an uncle wasn't exactly an earth-shattering revelation. And not talking about him until now was hardly a crime. Elodie had an uncle of her own that she and her family would rather like to pretend didn't exist. Unfortunately for them, he turned up every Christmas like a lump of coal in their Christmas stockings, and they all had to grin and bear him. But they had never tried to keep him a secret. 'It's not the fact that you've got an uncle that bothers me. It's that you've kept a secret from me. You know how much I dislike people keeping secrets. I thought I knew every single thing about you. It seems I was wrong. What else don't I know? What other secrets do you have that you haven't shared with me?'

'None!' Iris now looked a little hurt. 'You do know everything about me. Everything that matters, anyway. Everything that makes me, me. The only secret I have is Uncle Stanley. I mean *had*. The only secret I've ever had from you is ... was, him.'

That was the other part of the surprise revelation. Iris' Uncle Stanley was dead.

He'd actually died two days before, but Iris' dad, Frank Talbot, who was Stanley Talbot's brother – as Elodie had just found out – had only received the news today, via a telephone call from the family's solicitor, Arthur Cole.

Elodie knew who Arthur Cole was; she'd even met him a couple of times at some of the Talbot's 'Big Birthday' parties, and Frank and Sharon's milestone wedding anniversaries. Arthur wasn't just the family's solicitor; they considered him a friend. But not a close friend. Not a friend who would ring them on a Sunday afternoon, and they were surprised to get his call.

Frank had been on his way into the large open plan living room of their 1970s house, from the garden where he'd been digging the last of his carrots from inside one of the polytunnels in his beloved vegetable patch, when the landline phone rang. Sharon had been carrying in a tray of tea, coffee and some of her scrumptious shortbread, having called out to Frank to 'come and have a cuppa'. Iris and Elodie were sitting on the floor in front of a flame-effect gas fire, scrolling through recipes for festive cocktails via Iris' iPad.

Sharon had stopped in her tracks, the tray balanced in her hands, and Iris had jumped to her feet the moment Frank had answered the phone and said, 'Hello, Arthur. This is a surprise. Not bad news, I hope.' It was as if Sharon and Iris had known that this particular call from Arthur was something important. And probably something bad. Although they couldn't possibly have done so.

Frank had then apparently forgotten that Elodie had been in the room, possibly because, from where he stood, she was out of his line of sight, and had relayed to his wife and daughter what Arthur had said.

'Good grief, Sharon! Stanley's dead.'

'Dead?' Sharon had squealed, looking deathly pale herself. 'How can that be? He was only sixty-nine.'

Frank had shrugged, the deep frown almost cutting his forehead in two.

'Reverend Parker called round to see him yesterday morning, couldn't get a reply and decided to take a look through the sitting room window. He saw Stanley lying on the floor, and contacted the police. It's believed Stanley probably had a heart attack the previous day. No reason to suspect foul play. But then they clearly didn't know him. Arthur says there'll be a post mortem though, which is usually the case if someone dies unexpectedly at home. And Stanley wasn't exactly old. The police got in touch with Arthur because he was listed on Stanley's phone as his emergency contact. But that's not the only surprise. Arthur has just told me that the old bugger left everything to me.'

'Everything?' Iris had piped up, competing with her mum on the squeal-o-meter.

Frank had nodded. 'Everything.'

'Including Clementine Cottage?' his wife had asked, a smile creeping slowly across her mouth.

'Yep. Including Clementine Cottage.' Frank smiled too and the frown smoothed out to little more than a crinkle. 'He'd asked Arthur to draw up a will for him two months ago, leaving everything to me. Arthur was as surprised as we are but when Stanley went into his office to sign it, Arthur was certain Stanley was in full possession of all his faculties. He did ask Stanley about the sudden wish to make a will and why I was the only beneficiary. All Stanley said was something along the lines of, "We never know when our time will be up, and there's no one else to leave it to other than Frank." And that was it.'

'I'm so sorry for your loss,' Elodie had offered, feeling that she ought to say something at such a time, but wondering who this person was, and why none of the Talbots seemed particularly bothered by the news that he had passed away. In fact, they almost seemed ... pleased. She'd never heard of anyone called Stanley, and she knew all of the Talbot's friends and relations. Or she had thought she did. 'Was he a friend?'

Frank had looked askance and had stepped further into the room as if to check where the voice had come from.

'Ah, Elodie, my dear. I'd completely forgotten you were here. Um. Would you mind giving us an hour or two? Family business and all that, you know. Iris will come round and tell you ... er ... discuss it later.'

He'd held out his hand to her as if he was trying to hurry her along and, knowing when she wasn't wanted, Elodie got up off the floor. She'd known Frank and Sharon since the day she and Iris had become friends and the Talbots felt like Elodie's second family, so the fact that she was, effectively, being shut out made her feel a little hurt although she tried to not show it.

'Yes, of course. Are you okay, Iris?' she'd asked, as Frank ushered her towards the hall.

'What? Sorry. Yeah. I'll be round soon,' Iris called after her before Frank closed the front door.

Elodie was staying at her parents' house, two roads away from the Talbots, so she didn't have far to go, but the hour or so she had to wait until Iris rang the doorbell seemed like forever as she wondered who this Stanley was and why she'd never heard of him.

And when she did find out, she was even more surprised to discover that Iris had an uncle and he was called Stanley.

Iris told Elodie more about him. Stanley had been Frank's older brother, by ten years but there had been a rift and the Talbot family hadn't seen him, or spoken of him to anyone other than themselves, for at least thirty-six years.

Now he was dead.

But in spite of the rift and the fact that neither Iris nor her parents seemed upset, the man had apparently left Frank his entire estate, including some place called Clementine Cottage.

'And if I hadn't been there when the call came through, would you ever have told me about him?' Elodie queried, still scowling, as she and Iris sat at the table in Elodie's parents' kitchen.

Her parents were currently in Australia, visiting Elodie's elder sister, Sasha who had moved to Melbourne exactly one year ago after falling head over heels in love with an Aussie backpacker whom she'd met on a train eighteen months earlier and married not long after that.

Elodie should've gone with them, but just two days before the flight, her sitting room ceiling had landed on her brand new carpet, resulting in a sodden mass of white plaster, rotten timber and swamp-like pools of dirt, dust and insulation.

Unbeknown to Elodie, the roof had been leaking for many months, or so the roof repairer informed her, and after a week of nothing but torrential rain pouring through it and pooling on top of the ceiling, the thing had decided it could take no more.

She had been tempted to leave it and deal with it all when she came back, but she'd be gone for a month and that hadn't seemed a wise course of action, so she'd stayed behind to sort out the insurance and repairs, and planned to join her family later.

But by the time the place was almost back to the way it was before the ceiling had collapsed, it was hardly worth the trip. Her parents were coming back in less than one week and Elodie wasn't flying halfway around the world, cooped up on a plane for twenty-four hours, just to spend less than seven days with her sister and the family.

Luckily, the ticket, which was part of her Christmas present from her parents, was fully transferable. She'd go out in the summer, instead. Even though that would be Melbourne's winter and maybe not the best time for a visit.

Besides, the decorators were still at her place adding the finishing touches. Which was why she was still living at her parents' house and would stay there until her little terraced cottage was once again pristine.

Now Elodie was trying hard not to smile as the Christmas earrings Iris was wearing flashed on and off with every movement Iris made. They were little white fluffy snowmen with top hats, red noses and huge smiles and tiny LED lights flashed white and red alternately.

A weak smile tugged at Iris' mouth. 'Yes. I promise I would've told you. And as it happens. I need to ask you a favour.' The snowmen flashed like little warning signs.

'What? To keep this family skeleton of yours in the closet?'

Iris grinned at that. 'No. Although we'd rather it didn't become public knowledge, but now he's dead, it doesn't really matter who knows about him, I suppose. That wasn't the favour. Mum and Dad are going away on Tuesday, as you know. They can't cancel now, even if they wanted to – which they don't. This trip of theirs has been planned for ages and they're not giving it up just because Stanley's passed away. So they've asked me if I'd go and sort things out in Clementine Cove. You know. Make sure the cottage is locked up, and stuff like that.'

'Make sure the cottage is locked up?' Were they for real? Elodie could understand why Sharon and Frank didn't want to cancel their holiday. They were flying to Barbados on Tuesday and spending a few days there before boarding a cruise ship on Friday to sail around the Caribbean to celebrate their Ruby wedding anniversary. They'd be returning to London on Christmas Eve, landing at 5.50 a.m. on Christmas morning so that they could spend Christmas with their only daughter, Iris. They'd invited Iris to go with them, but she'd pulled a face, shaken her head and told them that, as much as she adored them there was no way she was going on holiday with her parents. No one would want to cancel such a special trip for someone they hadn't seen or spoken to for years, but surely, arranging the poor man's funeral should've been higher on the list of priorities than 'making sure the cottage was locked up'? 'Your uncle has just died. Your dad's brother. And all that matters to you and your parents is to make sure some cottage is locked up? Aren't you upset at all? What about your uncle? What about his funeral? Was your dad his only living relative?'

Iris frowned. 'I told you. Stanley was the black sheep of the family. I've never even met the man and Mum and Dad haven't spoken to him for more than thirty-six years. So no. Sorry. But we're not upset. Surprised, yes. Upset, no. Uncle Stanley wasn't a very nice man.'

'How do you know that? You said you never met him.'

Iris tutted. 'Because Mum and Dad told me who he was and what he was like.'

'And that was good enough for you? You didn't want to meet him and decide for yourself?'

'N-no. Why would I?'

Elodie sighed. 'Well, I would.'

'It's a bit too late for that,' Iris smirked.

'What was the reason for the rift? Or is that another secret?'

'Um …' Iris tilted her head to one side and her glossy red fringe fell across her forehead as her snowman earrings flashed on and off, this time while playing the tune of 'Frosty the Snowman', something extra they only seemed to do every now and then, or as Iris joked, 'whenever they could be bothered', but both she and Elodie ignored that. 'I honestly don't know. The reason for the rift, that is. Not whether it's a secret or not. Which I suppose it is. Or it was.'

'So what else haven't you told me?'

Iris shook her head and the snowmen danced on her shoulders. As much as Elodie loved Christmas, Iris' earrings were starting to get on her nerves.

'Nothing. I told you earlier, there's nothing else to tell.'

'No other secrets? No other relations I'm unaware of? No other skeletons in the closet?'

'No. None.' Iris grinned again. 'Well, none that you don't know about. Please don't be mad. It's not as if it's that important.'

'Not *that* important?' Elodie's voice raised several octaves.

'No. It really isn't. The man was as good as a stranger. And he was a complete stranger to me. Anyway. The favour I want to ask is ... will you come with me to Clementine Cove? We can go this weekend. Dad's made a few calls and I can pick up the keys on Friday morning. I could go earlier but I don't want to take that much time off work. I know it's the party season and it's a lot to ask, but your folks don't get back until next week and besides, I don't want to go on my own.'

Iris gave one of her smiles and it was hard for Elodie not to smile back. Iris had the sort of smile that made you want to do that, no matter how angry or hurt or upset you might be. Iris only had to smile and it made you feel that all was right with the world. Whether or not it was. And, of course, those annoying little snowmen were flashing smiles too.

'I'm still cross,' Elodie said, wagging a finger at her best friend. 'But fine. Just tell me one more thing. Where the hell is Clementine Cove? I've never heard of it. I won't need my passport, will I?'

Chapter 2

Clementine Cove was situated on a headland jutting out from the coastline of East Sussex, just a hair's breadth from the Kent border. The cove itself formed a large bay in the shape of a slightly squashed circle that looked as if it had been scooped out with a giant spoon from the expanse of rock and shingle cliffs that gave it shelter.

According to the internet, some people believed the village got its name from the fact that the cove looked like a clementine, sideways on, but legend had it that the cove was actually named after a famous witch who had once lived there and was said to have carved out the cove with a magic spell.

Or maybe, a magic spoon.

However it derived its name, Clementine Cove looked idyllic. The quintessential English village with narrow lanes bordered by wild flower and grass embankments on which colourful cottages sat as if they had burst up from the earth as some sort of giant flower. Some had thatched roofs, some had clay tiled roofs more than one hundred years old, and some had smart new tiles. There were even one or two with solar panels on the roofs, but according to one of the articles Elodie had read, they were regarded as somewhat *outré*.

The village had one pub and one church that stood facing one another on opposite sides of the sweep of the bay. To get to the church from the pub, you either had to walk all around the cliff, known as Clementine Drop, from Arrow Point until you reached Hope Head; a walk of almost two miles, or you could cross the mouth of the bay, which involved an often choppy boat trip, depending on the weather and sea conditions, of a quarter of a mile.

The local paper, the *Clementine Herald*, which had a mission statement of 'peeling back whatever it takes to find the truth' – a rather grandiose sentiment for a newspaper with a staff of three, had printed an article, unkindly stating that the residents of Clementine Cove usually went the other way: from the church to the pub, or that they took the 'slow' walk to the church and the 'fast' sail to the pub, especially after one of Reverend Wilfred Parker's frequently lengthy sermons. The paper received several acerbic missives after that, so the internet informed Elodie, but none from Reverend Parker himself – or none that were recorded in writing. Perhaps he preferred to 'turn the other cheek' but a later edition of the paper noted that his sermon the following week after the article appeared was a good ten minutes shorter than was usual.

Elodie read all that she could find about Clementine Cove, although there wasn't very much, and her time for research was cut short by the fact that it was only just over two weeks until Christmas and the party season was in full swing. Elodie loved a good party almost as much as she loved Christmas itself, and deciding what outfit to wear to each one took a considerable amount of time.

She'd only found out the place existed, on Sunday afternoon and she'd had a dinner party to attend on Sunday evening. Since then she'd been out every night and hard at work at her desk all day, running her family's online party store, which sold anything and everything anyone would possibly want or need to host the perfect party, large or small, adult or children's, tacky or sophisticated. Scouring the internet for information about Clementine Cove had naturally taken a back seat to that. Although she did have help running the business in her parents' absence. They had two other employees whom they had taken on when Elodie's sister had emigrated to Australia.

Now though, as Elodie sat in the passenger seat beside Iris on the journey from London to the village of Clementine Cove, she read everything she could.

'It says here that a new housing estate was built at the edge of the village ten years ago and that the locals were all up in arms about it. And looking at this map, it seems that the estate is just the other side of your uncle's cottage with only a row of trees and a fence dividing them. Look.' She held out her phone but Iris waved it away.

'I'm driving, El. I can't look at it now. I told you we should've waited until the rain stopped. I can hardly see a thing and these bloody wipers may be doing their best, but frankly it's just not good enough.'

Iris was a voice coach and she had exacting standards which she often applied to things other than merely her private clients. She started her career as a singing teacher but after several requests, both from blue chip companies and private individuals, she now also trained people to use their voice to its full potential in order to make powerful, impressive and impactful speeches, presentations and such.

Like Elodie, Iris worked from home, which meant that neither had to concern themselves with 'office hours', just with their own business needs.

Elodie grinned at Iris before peering through the windscreen at the sheet-like rain.

'The forecast says the weather's going to get worse, so if we'd waited until the rain stopped, we might not have come until next week. Besides, it's not as if it's a major excursion. It's only sixty miles and we're more than halfway there already. It won't be long until we're indoors with a glass of eggnog, or a hot chocolate.' She whipped her head around to look at Iris again. 'The cottage does have heating doesn't it?'

Iris glanced across at her briefly, and shrugged. 'How should I know? I've never been to the place, and Dad only went there a few times and that was when he was a kid. It was owned by an aunt but she left the place to Stanley when she died. It could be falling down for all I know. You're the one who's been trawling the web for photos and stuff. Haven't you found any pictures of the cottage? Not that they would show if it had central heating.'

Elodie shook her head. 'Only an aerial shot, which isn't much use. The cottage is surrounded by fields and trees so I suppose the camera-thingy that takes the street photos couldn't get a good view of it. The aerial shot did show that the place has a roof though, so that's a good thing.' She laughed and Iris laughed too.

'I should hope so. Uncle Stanley's been living there for most of his adult life, from what Mum and Dad have said, and although I don't really know anything about him, from the things I've heard them say, he was a man who liked his home comforts. So I suppose that answers your question. Yes. I'm sure the cottage will have heating.'

'Phew. That's a relief. I'm still shivering from that weekend away I went on with Rubin. And that was three weeks ago.'

Iris laughed louder. 'You've only got yourself to blame for that. You knew he was the 'outdoorsy' type. You're lucky there was a caravan in those woods – albeit one that had clearly been abandoned years before. I heard he usually just pitches a tent when he goes away for his 'wilderness weekends'.'

'He did pitch a tent. I told you that, and that I slept in the caravan. I thought I'd died and gone to hell when I woke up.' She shivered dramatically.

'Hmm. I wonder why that relationship didn't last?'

Elodie and Iris could joke about Rubin and about most, if not all, of the other men each of them had dated. But since her ex-fiancé had broken her heart five years before, what Elodie couldn't seem to do was find a man with whom she could have a real and lasting relationship.

But then again, neither could Iris. And no man had ever broken Iris' heart. Iris had always been the one to end all of her relationships.

Elodie gave her a playful slap. 'Don't be sarcastic. It was a shame though. He was really handsome. And fit. But when he asked me if I'd like to spend a weekend in the country with him, I'd pictured a cosy inn, or a B&B, or, if I'm honest, one of those posh country house hotels. What was the guy thinking? I mean, do I look like the type of woman who likes being knee-deep in mud and sleeping on wet ground?'

Iris pulled up at a crossroads and looked Elodie up and down, grinning broadly.

'I think your perfectly tonged 'hot auburn' waves with those gold and chestnut lowlights, not to mention the glitter in your hair, the immaculate make-up and glistening red lips that match the sparkly red and silver nail polish you're wearing as a result of an obviously expensive day at Bella's Beauty Rooms, would indicate not.' She rolled her eyes and laughed. 'But men are a different breed. And some of them aren't very bright when it comes to stuff like that. Rubin may have been an impressive sight for any woman's eyes, but he hadn't a clue what a woman might like.'

'And you wouldn't guess that, because I was partying all night, all this glamour was left over from yesterday, would you? Last night was great. You really should've come.'

'And miss my date with the delectable Danny? Not on your life.'

'Giving a singing lesson to a heart-throb actor is not a date, Iris.'

Iris threw her a sardonic smile. 'It is in my world. I haven't had a real date since ... Oh blimey! It's been so long I can't even remember.'

'I remember. It was three months ago and it was with that awful guy with halitosis, bad enough to be classed as an act of terrorism every time he opened his mouth. I still don't know why you went out for a drink with him, although to be fair, I suppose you couldn't possibly have known about his breath as you'd only spoken to him on the phone.'

To this day, Elodie couldn't believe that Iris had made a date with a guy who had cold-called her to sell her double glazing. Iris had liked the guy's voice; they'd chatted and joked and after thirty minutes, and having established that the guy had blond hair and blue eyes, Iris had asked him on a date.

When she'd told Elodie about it, Elodie had insisted on being at the wine bar where they'd arranged to meet.

'He could be a serial killer, or something. Or even worse. He could be a liar, a cheat and a total bastard ... like Ben.'

Ben Lincoln was Elodie's ex-fiancé – and the reason why she hated people keeping secrets. He'd kept a huge secret from her for almost two years and it had broken her heart when she had finally discovered the truth.

That had been five years ago and it still cut her in two every time she thought about him, or mentioned his name, or compared him to any of her subsequent boyfriends, which she always did, no matter how hard she tried not to.

Ben Lincoln had been the life of her life.

Unfortunately for her, his secret proved he hadn't felt the same.

And as Iris liked to point out, it also proved she had appalling taste in men.

Iris screwed up her face. 'Oh yeah. Quickly moving on. Were there any decent guys at the party last night?'

'None worth staying sober for. But it was a great party, as I said.'

Elodie yawned. She wouldn't admit it to anyone other than Iris but although she'd had a fantastic time at one of their other friend's office Christmas party, she was getting a bit old for all night parties, especially ones where she was dancing for most of the night and early hours of the morning, and drinking until dawn.

She couldn't quite remember how, or when, she'd made it home to her parents' house, but she woke with a start, still fully clothed and her make up surprisingly intact, but with her hair stuck to her cheek, when Iris had rung her doorbell as if there was a fire in the house.

Elodie had enough time for a quick wash, and a change of clothes; Iris assuring her she could have a shower later. She threw on some jeans, her favourite black thigh length boots, and a Christmas-themed red jumper, bolted down the cup of coffee Iris had kindly made while waiting for her, and tossed a couple of clementines from the fruit bowl into her handbag.

Luckily, she had packed her weekend bag the evening before, so all she had to do was pick that up from the hall where she'd left it ready and waiting for the ungodly hour that Iris had told her to be ready.

Not that 8 a.m. was early. Elodie had always been an early riser. But 8 a.m. after an all-nighter, was nothing short of hell. 'I am feeling a bit knackered now though. Would you mind if I nodded off for a bit?'

Iris laughed and shook her head as she turned left onto another B-road.

'Be my guest. I'll wake you when we get there. But no snoring, okay?'

'Snoring? Me?' Elodie shifted in the seat, lowering the seat back slightly so that she could get really comfy. 'I don't snore. That is a foul and untrue rumour. You're the one who does that.'

She grinned at Iris. The truth was, they both snored, and in less than five minutes, she knew she would be snoring like a steam engine.

Chapter 3

Clementine Cove was made up of two distinct areas: the old and the new, or so it had seemed on screen, and as Elodie and Iris drove past the sign welcoming them to the village and asking them to 'drive carefully and enjoy your stay in England's prettiest cove', the first area they saw was the new shopping centre called Millside, which was pretty, in a theme-park sort of way.

Elodie had read that one of the largest ever windmills in the UK had once stood proud on the site, but it had been razed to the ground in a terrible fire, way back in the 1880s and it had never been rebuilt.

When developers applied for permission to build a new shopping arcade on the old site, the local council, in its questionable wisdom, had insisted on a replica mill being erected, and a water wheel added for good measure.

The former, natural pond had been expanded to twice its original size and was now called Millside Lake, a small part of which wasn't a lake at all, but a manmade platform, designed to look as if some of the water had been sectioned off by a circular, wooden board walk. In the summer, this area was used for roller skating and skateboarding but at this time of year, with the addition of synthetic ice panels, it became an ice-skating rink encircled by a winter wonderland of snow-covered Christmas trees.

There was also a little river that began at the new lake and wound its way through the shopping centre and back to the lake again. A bit like a moat – only not.

The outside of the centre was painted black and white and although it was currently festooned with Christmas decorations and massive festive wreaths, none of the lights were switched on at this time of day and in the torrential rain, it actually looked a little bleak and not all that welcoming. The inside was no doubt, a different story and Elodie would be persuading Iris to pay Millside shopping centre a visit during this weekend.

Most of the photos Elodie had seen were taken in the spring or summer, but once they had driven past Millside, even now, with many of the trees bare, and hardly one flower to be seen in the grass verges, Clementine Cove oozed charm.

The village itself was approached by a steep hill, from the top of which there was a view right across the bay and out to sea. Not that Elodie could really see the sea as it melded into the grey sky and it was impossible to tell where one ended and the other began. But she could make out the edge of the land, and a lighthouse that stood on a large isle-like rock, just offshore, its beam flashing like a beacon of warmth as it spun around in the persistent torrential rain.

'I can see the lighthouse,' she said, pointing at it in the distance. 'And the tower of the church. So that must be the pub on that rocky promontory opposite. So ... working backwards from there, across the bay, I think I can make out the roof of Clementine Cottage. Look!'

Iris laughed. 'I think you're more excited about seeing the place than I am. You sound like a kid at Christmas.'

'I am excited. Don't ask me why. But it's a bit of an adventure, isn't it?'

'I suppose so.'

At the foot of Pound Road, they drove around Moneymaker Circle, a roundabout with a gigantic Douglas Fir tree at its centre. The tree was covered in multi-coloured lights that twinkled brightly, having been left switched on, possibly to provide some cheer on such a grey, wet day.

'That tree's so pretty,' Elodie said, before spotting the new housing estate on her left where many of the modern houses had a plethora of festive lights of their own.

'It's certainly very Christmassy,' Iris added as she turned onto Wayfarer's Road and then took a left into Middle Cut, passing pastel-fronted cottages more tastefully decorated.

They turned right onto Clementine Avenue, at which point the rain suddenly stopped, and finally, left onto Clementine Way, which was little more than a narrow tarmac track leading to Clementine Cottage and an area for parking two or possibly three cars.

'Wow!' said Iris as she pulled up outside the terracotta-coloured brick cottage. 'It's much grander looking than I expected.'

'It's beautiful,' Elodie said, taking in the two chimneys, the red roof tiles, the white painted wood surrounds of the Georgian windows, the porch that appeared to be leaning slightly to the right and the solid but welcoming, sunshine yellow front door with its large, black wrought iron handle. It was a pity it didn't have even a single Christmas decoration in place, but it was still two weeks until Christmas Day and maybe Stanley Talbot left his Christmas decorating until later. Or at least he would have perhaps, if he hadn't just died.

Elodie and Iris exchanged excited glances and, as the sun peeped out from the clouds which scudded away revealing a silvery-blue sky, they smiled at each other.

'It's a sign,' Iris said. 'I think this is going to be more fun than I expected.'

They shoved open the car doors and stepped out onto the tarmac at exactly the same time, but the stiff breeze wasn't quite so welcoming.

Elodie's hair whipped her face and Iris' flashing earrings, this time, Nutcrackers – danced like drunken ballerinas. In the bay, that was closer than it had looked on the map, sail ropes clattered against masts on boats bobbing in the marina, a few of which were just visible from where Elodie and Iris stood shivering. Gulls squawked and circled above, some swooping so close to one another their wingtips almost touched, some squabbling and some just seemingly drifting on the breeze.

'It's freezing!' Elodie exclaimed, watching them and hoping they didn't bomb her and Iris with their foul-smelling poo. Some people said that brought good luck, but

Elodie didn't want to find out. 'Where have we got to go to get the keys?'

'The rectory. It's called Rosehip Cottage and it's at the end of Church Lane, right by the church. I've got the vicar's number so I'll call him and tell him we're here. He said it was only a few minutes' walk across the fields, but the church looks farther away than a few minutes and those fields look more like quagmires, so we'd probably be best to double back the way we came and drive to the rectory, because we can't get to it from here, other than by foot.'

Elodie merely nodded and they both got back in the car where Iris switched on the ignition and turned the heater to full blast.

Elodie laughed. 'That was ... invigorating. Is it just me or does it feel twice as cold down here as it did in London?'

'It's not just you.' Iris shivered dramatically. 'That was definitely nippy. Thank heavens the rain stopped though.' She dialled the number for Reverend Parker and he answered within seconds. 'Hi. It's Iris Talbot. My friend and I are at the cottage. We're going to drive round to the rectory now, if that's okay with you.'

Elodie could hear the vicar's reply even though the phone wasn't on speaker.

'Hello, my dear! Welcome to Clementine Cove. I hope you had a pleasant journey.

You're welcome to come and say hello, but I did leave a key under the third flowerpot on the left. I decided it might be best, bearing in mind the weather was rather unpleasant today, and you'd probably be tired after your journey. Although the sun has just come out, I see. Why don't you let yourselves in, and my dear sister and I will pop round to you?'

Iris shot a look at Elodie. 'Oh. Thank you. Er. There's really no need for you and your sister to come round if you've left a key. It's freezing out. We'll be fine.'

'But ... you don't know where anything is, my dear. It's really no trouble. We're used to this weather.'

'No. Honestly. We'll find everything we need. And if we can't, we'll give you a call. We're pretty tired after driving so far in mostly torrential rain, so if you don't mind, we'll settle ourselves in and relax a bit before saying our hellos.'

'Oh. Yes, of course. Do call if you need us though. And if not, we'll pop round later to welcome you properly. Or you could join us for lunch?'

'No! Um. Thanks. I don't mean to be rude or anything but we're only here for today and the weekend and we've got a lot to do. We will drop by and see you though. When we get a chance. Thanks for the key. You have a good day. Bye.'

Iris rang off and let out a sigh.

Elodie laughed. 'For someone not meaning to be rude, you were pretty rude.'

'Did you want to have lunch with a vicar and his – did he say sister?'

Elodie nodded. 'He did. So obviously no wife. And no. I didn't want to have lunch with them. Right. Let's get inside and see what your uncle's taste in furnishing is like. Was like.' She opened the car door once again and walked around to Iris, falling into step beside her as they headed past a somewhat rickety looking post and rail, wood fence that had definitely seen better days, down an equally old, brick path, towards the front door. 'Third flowerpot on the left, the vicar said. He was really loud, wasn't he? I wonder if that's because he needs to speak loudly for his sermons.'

'No. He was just shouting. Some people do that on the phone. Especially older people. And he sounded old, didn't he?'

'Ancient. I would like to see what he looks like. I've already got a mental picture in my head.'

Iris laughed. 'Me too. But if I tell you, you'll say I'm being rude.'

Elodie grinned at her. 'Short and dumpy, I'd say. Balding on top, and those half-moon glasses perched on the end of a stubby, red nose.'

'And his sister will look just like him. Except she'll have round rimmed glasses and a mop of grey, curly hair.'

'With pearls, a handknitted cardigan, a floral dress, thick tights and sensible shoes.'

Iris raised one brow. 'The vicar? Or his sister?'

They both laughed at that as Iris bent down and lifted the third flowerpot to the left of the front door and felt around for the key.

She gave Elodie a frustrated glance before lifting the pot in the air with both hands. 'Is it there, El? Can you see the key?'

Elodie quickly bent down and looked. 'Nope. Nothing. But I'm sure that's what he said. Third flowerpot to the left.' She furrowed her brows in thought as Iris lowered the pot back into position. 'Unless he meant his left. You know. From where he was standing when you spoke to him. Let's check the third flowerpot on the right.'

Iris let out a sigh and followed Elodie. 'Fine. But you're lifting this one. Those things are heavier than they look.'

'That's because they're clay, not plastic.' Elodie bent down and tilted the pot to one side. 'Anything?'

'Nope.'

Elodie twisted the pot back and forth on its edge, gradually moving it away. Iris was right. The pot was heavy, and this one was twice the size of the one Iris had lifted.

'Now?'

'Nope. Apart from a family of woodlice that you've just made homeless.'

Elodie settled the pot back on the ground. 'Well then. Either the vicar lied, or his memory is failing him.'

'Damn. I suppose that means we'll have to drive round to the rectory, after all.'

They walked back to the car but as they were about to get in, Elodie spotted two figures coming across the fields from the direction of the church, and possibly, the rectory, and hurrying towards the cottage.

'Or maybe not.' She nodded in the direction of the people. 'Look.'

Iris turned around and a moment later she glanced at Elodie with a look of astonishment.

'If that's the vicar and his sister, both of us were completely wrong.'

Chapter 4

'Hello again!' a tall, slim and remarkably handsome, grey-haired man called out, who was racing towards Elodie and Iris beside an equally tall, slim and stunning redhead who looked so similar she was obviously a close relative. They were both dressed from head to toe in black Lycra running gear which had long yellow reflective stripes down each side and around every hem. The outfits left little to the imagination and outlined every curve, angle and muscle of their clearly super-fit bodies. The pair were sprinting at a speed that would make an Olympic runner seem tardy and when they came to a rapid halt a moment later, neither were even slightly out of breath. 'I'm so very sorry, my dear.'

'You're Reverend Wilfred Parker?' Iris' astonishment was evident in her tone.

He nodded and his warm smile gave way to perfect, white teeth as he held out his hand. 'I am. I apologise for the way we're dressed but we'd just returned home from a ten-mile run, when you phoned. You must be Iris. I can see the resemblance to Stanley.'

Iris' face fell as they shook hands. 'Thanks.'

The woman beside him laughed but there was a definite edge to it and to her voice when she spoke.

'That's a compliment. Stanley was an extremely good-looking man. But you wouldn't know that, I don't suppose. I believe you'd never met him. Hi. I'm Will's sister. My name's Rosamunde but everyone calls me Rosie.'

'Hi,' Iris said. 'And you're right. We never met. This is my best friend, Elodie.'

'Pleased to meet you both,' Elodie said, taking an instant dislike to Rosie. Who wore full make-up, including lipstick, to go running? And how come the woman could look so good after running ten miles – and in the rain? And why didn't either of them need coats? Or at the very least, running jackets. It was absolutely freezing.

'Here.' Wilfred held a bunch of keys in his other hand and he passed the keys to Iris. 'I can only apologise again. My memory isn't what it was. I was planning to leave a key beneath the flowerpot this morning, and in fact, I thought I had. But Rosie reminded me we'd discussed it and decided against it after yesterday.'

'What happened yesterday?' Iris shot a quick look at Elodie.

'Nothing to worry you, I'm sure. But we didn't want to take any chances. Marian called us yesterday. Oh that's Marian Blythe of Cove Café. You can just see a glimpse of the café from here. It's that ruby coloured cottage on the end of Cove Close.' He pointed it out and Iris and Elodie nodded. 'She saw someone "sneaking around" to use her words. Now, we're both certain she was probably mistaken because Clementine Cove is a safe place to live and crime rates here are virtually non-existent, but by now, people have heard of dear Stanley's passing, and well, as Rosie here reminded me, it's better to be safe than sorry, I suppose. So although I had intended to leave you a key, I hadn't. Sorry.'

'Someone was sneaking around?' Elodie didn't like the sound of that.

Rosie laughed and dismissively waved a hand in the air. 'Marian's a bit of a drama queen, between you and me. I'd normally take anything she said with a pinch of salt. As Will said, this place is one of the safest in the UK, but since the new housing estate was built...' She shook her head and sighed loudly. 'Well. One can't be too careful. I told

Will I felt it might be wiser to err on the side of caution, that's all.'

'I see,' Iris said, looking worried in spite of the reassurances. 'Okay. Thanks for bringing over the keys. We'd probably better get started. Lots to do.'

'Would you like us to show you where everything is, as we're here?' Wilfred's smile was hopeful.

Iris shook her head decisively. 'No need. Really. We'll be fine. Besides, you and Rosie must be freezing. You haven't even got jackets.'

Wilfred and Rosie exchanged glances.

'We don't feel the cold,' Rosie said.

'Running keeps us warm,' Wilfred added.

'But you're not running now,' said Iris.

'We're freezing,' Elodie said, emphasizing the point by shivering. 'It's lovely to meet you but if you don't mind, Iris and I do feel the cold, so we want to get inside and get warm. We'll possibly see you again over the weekend.' She moved towards the door and nodded her head to Iris who did the same.

'Yeah. Thanks again. See you around.'

'Will we see you in church on Sunday?' Wilfred asked, the smile not so warm now.

'Church?' Iris made it sound as if she had no idea what a church was. 'No. Sorry.'

Rosie stiffened visibly. 'Stanley was a regular. He was also in the choir. He had the voice of an angel.'

'Iris has the voice of a tone-deaf duck,' Elodie lied. 'As do I. You're better off without us.'

Iris gave her an odd look but it quickly turned to gratitude and she smiled as she added, 'And we're only here for the weekend.'

Elodie wasn't sure why she had lied; the words just tumbled out. She was freezing and she wanted to get inside. If the vicar and his sister knew Iris had the voice of a choir of angels, not just one angel, they'd probably have tried to persuade her to sing in their choir or something. Even worse, if they discovered she taught people how to sing, they might've asked her to give some of the choir free coaching. It wouldn't be the first time that had happened.

'So you said.' Rosie's eyes narrowed momentarily, her heavy black lashes moving closer together, like a spider creeping up on a fly about to get tangled in its web. 'We'll let you get on then. You know where to find us. We hope you enjoy your stay. Come along, Will. Let's leave them to it.'

'Oh. Er. Okay.' Wilfred's disappointment was evident in his tone and on his face. 'Don't forget to call if you need us. We're only five minutes' walk away. Two, if you run.

Goodbye for now. I'll pop round before you leave.'

'Why?' Iris was at the door and had inserted the key in the lock. 'I mean. There's no need. We'll take the keys back with us.'

'Don't you want to leave one here, just in case?'

'Of what? I thought you said it was the safest place in the UK?'

'It is. It's also winter, my dear. And winter means frozen pipes and such like. With the cottage empty, I assumed your family would want someone to pop in every now and then to check everything was all right. Rosie and I would be happy to do that.'

'Ah. Thanks for the offer. I'll discuss it with my mum and dad and let you know. I think we might be selling the place so we'll give the agents a key if we do.'

'Selling the place?' Rosie sounded shocked. 'Stanley would hate that.'

'Sadly, Stanley's no longer around,' Iris said. 'We all live in London. My parents may decide to keep it as a holiday home, or maybe rent it out. Nothing's been decided yet. But it makes more sense to sell. Bye.' Iris shoved the front door open, grabbed the sleeve of Elodie's coat, and hurried them both inside, closing the door firmly behind her and leaning her back against it as if to prevent invaders. 'I thought we'd never get away from them.' She puffed out a sigh of relief. 'Thanks for lying about my voice. I know exactly why you did that.'

'Who said I was lying?' Elodie grinned. 'They were nothing like I expected. In fact, I'd say they were both the complete opposite of how I imagined them.'

'Tell me about it! And pushy, don't you think? They seemed very keen to come in, didn't they?'

'Yeah. But I'm not sure why. They've had the keys for a few days now, haven't they? They could've been in and out of here as often as they wanted.'

'That's true,' Iris acknowledged. 'Perhaps they really did just want to show us around. But I have no idea why. I mean. It's a cottage, not a stately home.'

'It's much larger than I thought it'd be,' said Elodie, looking around her.

The hall was as wide as the porch and surprisingly bright and airy with a pale but warm terracotta wash on the walls, and a white wash on the wood floor which had an ancient looking, ornately patterned but almost threadbare runner down the long length of it. This front hall opened up into a wider, rear hall with a flight of unpainted wood and equally ancient looking stairs to one side. There was also a large, glass panelled white washed wood door with two half-sized windows either side of it, one above the lower half of the stairs and one above a grey table bearing a vase of dried woodland foliage. Four doors, all painted white and currently all closed, led off the hall and several framed photographs hung at various angles between each one.

'This isn't what I expected either,' Iris said, matching Elodie's own thoughts.

'Nothing seems to be,' Elodie said. 'The vicar and his sister look like a cross between Greek gods and retired Olympians, and this place, so far, looks as if it's right out of one of those magazines about country homes, your mum always reads. I think I expected it to be dark and gloomy for some reason.'

'Same here. Perhaps the rooms are.' Iris opened the first door and looked inside. 'Nope.'

She shoved it wide open to reveal a light, bright sitting room, once again with a whitewashed floor, but this time covered with a thicker, newer and plain deep ruby-red, large rug. The two sofas and two armchairs were almost identical in colour and scattered with flora and fauna patterned cushions, which the curtains at the two large windows matched, as did the cushions on the window seats. There was a large fireplace with a massive fire basket that was currently filled with remnants of wood and ash from the last fire that had blazed there.

'Wow!' Elodie said. 'I can already see us curled up in our PJs in front of a real, log fire, drinking hot chocolate and scoffing mince pies, can't you? After we've hung Christmas stockings from that mantle which we'd have dressed with garlands of holly, ivy and mistletoe, and more than a few pine cones, collected from walks in the woods. There'd be a Christmas tree in that corner, decorated to within an inch of its life and surrounded by piles of beautifully wrapped presents. Festive cushions and throws on the window seats and tasteful decorations placed wherever there's a space.'

Iris nodded. 'Uncle Stanley might not have been a nice man but he had good taste.'

'Yeah. About that. The vicar and his sister seem to have been friends of your uncle. Do you think that maybe, either he wasn't as bad as you thought, or that he had, perhaps, changed over the years and turned into a nice guy?'

Iris shrugged. 'Don't know. And it's a bit too late to find out.'

'It's not. You could ask the locals about him. We already know he had two friends ... possibly. Two very good-looking and fit friends, no less. We know he went to church and sang in the choir. Not that that makes him a good guy, of course, but it does indicate he was involved with the community. It might be fun to find out more about him, don't you think?'

Iris nodded. 'Yeah. It might. It certainly can't do any harm.'

She headed towards the door opposite, opening it into another bright and welcoming room. This was the dining room and had a long oblong table with eight chairs neatly positioned around it, all with velvet padded seats in the same deep ruby-red, an antique sideboard, an equally old, glass cabinet filled with glasses and crockery, and another open fire and large mantle. The two windows had the same curtains and window seat cushions as those in the sitting room.

'I think I'm falling in love with this place,' Elodie said, following Iris into the room and pulling out one of the chairs. 'Imagine having Christmas dinner around this table. There'd be candelabra amongst festive foliage running down the centre. A roaring log fire in that hearth, with even more Christmas stockings hanging from the festively decorated mantle. Another tree in that corner, maybe smaller than the one in the sitting room but still generously decorated. More festive cushions and throws on the window seats, oh, and fairy lights at all the windows. I forgot those in the sitting room. But I suppose it goes without saying there'd be lights. Lots of lights.'

Iris laughed. 'It's you, El. Of course that goes without saying. You alone keep the fairy light industry going.' Iris pulled out a chair opposite and sat at the table, running her hand over the top of the polished surface and turning her palm towards Elodie. 'Look at that. Hardly a speck of dust. We know another thing about Stanley. Either he did his own housework or he had a cleaner. Both rooms are spotless, aren't they? There's not even a hint of anything out of place.'

'I wonder if every room is like that?'

'Let's go and see.'

Iris got up and hurried to the next door. It opened into a large country kitchen complete with a central, old pine table, a dresser stacked with crockery and ornaments, a butler's sink, and pale blue fitted kitchen units with marbled granite worktops to three sides, on top of which sat several deep red kitchen appliances. Two large windows, again with window seats, looked out on to a garden filled with trees and shrubs and well maintained lawns.

'Look!' Elodie shrieked. 'There's a fox.'

She rushed to the window and, kneeling on the window seat, peered out, half expecting the fox to flee, but it sat down and stared straight back at her.

'It's beautiful,' Iris said, joining her on the window seat. 'I think that's the first time I've ever seen a fox so close up. I know there's supposed to be loads running the streets at home, but I've never seen one like this.'

'There's another one!'

Iris tipped her head to one side and stuck a finger in her ear. 'Thanks for that. I think I've just gone deaf. I'm right beside you, El. There's no need to scream the place down.'

Elodie laughed and nudged her friend's arm. 'Sorry. I couldn't help it. I love foxes. You know I do. I was excited to see one, but two. This is ... it's a Christmas miracle!'

Iris laughed at that. 'Hardly a miracle. We're in the countryside. I expect we'll see lots of foxes and badgers and hedgehogs and stuff. And look. Now there's a robin on that fence post. All we need now is snow and we'll have more than a Christmas miracle. We'll have a real-life Christmas card.'

Elodie pulled out her phone and took a stream of photos, disappointed when both foxes eventually turned away and, seemingly playing some sort of game of tag, ran off into the trees, followed almost immediately by the robin.

'Show's over,' Iris said. 'Let's see the rest of this place.'

The last room on the ground floor was locked and Iris had to try each of the eight keys on the bunch until she found the one that opened it.

'It's a study,' Elodie said, taking in the antique desk in the middle of the room, the red leather and oak, captain's chair, the neatly stacked pile of papers on shelves and racks, the pens in pots, and a single plant at one corner of the desk, just behind a closed laptop which sat at the centre.

Again, the two windows in this room had window seats and the same style and pattern of curtains and cushions, and there were three old wooden filing cabinets to one side of the room with a smaller fireplace with a log burning stove to the other.

'I wonder why he had a study?' Iris said.

'Perhaps he still worked and he did it from home. Did your parents know what he did for a living?'

Iris shook her head. 'They didn't say and I didn't think to ask.' She went to the desk and switched on the laptop but once it had gone through its rapid wakeup a big square popped up asking for the password. 'No idea what that is.' She switched it off and closed the lid 'Let's look at this later. It doesn't really matter now what he did.'

'I suppose not.' Elodie shivered. 'I know this sounds weird ... but ... there's something about this room. Don't ask me what. It's just a feeling.'

'You and your 'feelings'. It's probably the cold. When we first came in, it felt warm compared to outside. Now it's beginning to feel cold in here. Maybe we should find out how to turn the heating on before we venture upstairs. I've seen a radiator in every room and there's one in the hall, so we just need to find the boiler and the thermostat control and get some warmth into this place.'

'Good idea. And maybe light a fire or two in those hearths. Have you ever made a fire? I haven't.'

'Nope. But we've both had barbeques and we've lit those. It's probably much the same.'

The boiler was in a small utility room to one side of the kitchen. They hadn't noticed it at first as the door looked like a kitchen unit but when Iris commented on the size of the red, free standing American-style fridge, Elodie wondered what was behind the large cupboard door. It could've been another fridge freezer in a built-in unit but when she opened it, she discovered what it was.

'There's a utility room here, Iris. Look. And there's the boiler.'

They turned the boiler on without difficulty and set the timer situated to the right of it, leaving it on until 10 p.m. that night.

'I don't suppose the heating's been on much since ... they found him,' Iris said. 'We'll keep it on today and see how warm it gets. Let's leave the fires till we've had a look around upstairs.'

There was a hall at the top of the stairs, similar to the ground floor hall and they soon discovered three beautifully decorated bedrooms, each with window seats, antique furniture and large, comfy-looking beds with intricately designed wooden bedframes; they all had sumptuous bedspreads made of velvet – a different colour for each room. One was a midnight blue, one was a rich yellow gold, and one was the same deep red as the furniture downstairs. Each had soft furnishings to match and enhance its colour palette.

The fourth door off this hallway was a massive bathroom with an original roll top cast iron bath on ball and claw feet, set in front of one of the two windows which had privacy glass dotted with several clear spots – so not that private, really. There was a modern walk-in shower and rainfall showerhead opposite the bath. The sink was in front of the other window with the toilet situated on the other side of the sink.

Elodie grinned. 'Your uncle could sit on the loo and then wash his hands, all the while peeking through the clear spots on the panes, and laze in the bath and look at the stars.'

'Have you noticed there are window seats, and in this case a toilet seat and a bath, positioned in front of every window in this cottage?'

'Yeah. I noticed that too.'

'He obviously liked to look out at the view.'

'Perhaps he loved watching the wildlife. Maybe he loved foxes as much as I do.'

'Or the locals. Maybe he liked watching people coming and going. You can see half the village, if not all of it, from various rooms in this cottage.'

Elodie let out a soft sigh as they made their way back downstairs. 'Maybe he was lonely.'

'Maybe he was nosy.'

'You're determined to think the worst of him, aren't you?'

Iris shrugged, her Nutcracker earrings leaping about on her shoulders. 'I can't help it. Mum and Dad never had a good word to say about him. Not that they talked much of him. I suppose I just think of him as a nasty, unpleasant sort of man.'

'Well, why don't we go to that café the vicar and Rosie mentioned, and see what other people thought of him? I could murder a coffee right now. Or better still, a hot chocolate. Maybe even a slice of cake or a mince pie. We can unpack and sort this place out later. And it'll give the heating time to do its job. What do you say?'

'I say, why are we still standing here? Let's go.'

Chapter 5

Cove Café was probably only a couple of minutes' walk across the garden of Clementine Cottage and the field beyond but both the garden and the field looked more like green lakes than lawns and grass fields right now and neither Elodie nor Iris were wearing the appropriate footwear. Their leather, thigh length boots, which were identical apart from Elodie's being black and Iris' being purple, had stiletto heels, perfect for parading along Kensington High Street, their favourite shopping haunt, or for nights out drinking in their local pubs and wine bars, but completely useless for navigating muddy gardens and fields.

Besides, it was far too cold to walk, especially as that part of the garden and the surrounding field opened directly onto the cliff above the bay and the choppy, windswept sea beyond. Even from inside the hall they could hear the wind whistling around the cottage and rattling the windows and the front and back doors.

Walking to the café via the roads would probably only take an additional five minutes, but they decided the moment they opened the front door, even that was too long in such weather. The rain might have stopped but although the sun was doing its best, it gave little warmth and no protection from the blustery and increasingly icy wind which had grown stronger since Elodie and Iris had been inside Clementine Cottage.

'Let's take the car,' Iris said, decisively. 'I can see from here that there's ample parking on the road outside the café.'

'Unless it's double lines,' Elodie pointed out. 'But I can't see any road markings from here.'

'There's only one way to find out.'

They dashed to the car and Iris drove to the café, pulling up right outside. There were no parking notices or road markings to be seen, but neither were there any other cars on Cove Close, which seemed a little odd. There had been cars parked elsewhere though so at least the village wasn't a car-free zone. Perhaps the occupants of the cottages and shops on this road simply didn't own cars.

From the outside, Cove Café looked like a family home. Only the menu pasted inside one of the windows and a delicious-looking display of Christmas cakes, mince pies, cinnamon swirls and a range of seemingly edible Santas, reindeers and elves, together with the faint but heady aromas of freshly brewed coffee, and bread just out of the oven, gave a clue as to what it actually was.

Elodie opened the pale pink front door, careful not to disturb the massive Christmas wreath covering a large section of it, and stepped inside the café. As she did so, the first line of the song, Jingle Bells burst out from beneath her feet.

Iris laughed and pointed at the doormat. It had a picture of a very jolly Father Christmas ringing two handheld bells and beside him was a reindeer with a row of bells and coloured fairy lights strung around its antlers. The tune played again the moment Iris stepped on it, and this time Elodie laughed too whilst the fairy lights on the reindeer flashed on and off.

'We need one of these for the cottage,' Iris said, still laughing.

'Some people like it, some people hate it,' a friendly voice said. 'You can get them from the Christmas Market In the Millside centre. It's there every day until Christmas, including Christmas Eve.'

Elodie and Iris looked at the woman walking towards them. She was about the same age as them – mid-thirties, or maybe a little older, slim and exceedingly pretty. She had dark brown, almost chocolate-coloured, wavy hair and was wearing a set of felt antlers as a headband. Her apron appeared to be the body of a reindeer, holding a pen in one of its hooves and a long, curled list bearing names, some with ticks and others with crosses beside them, in the other. It was obviously meant to be Santa's naughty and nice list. The woman gave them a warm and friendly smile.

'We love it,' Elodie said. 'And your apron.'

'Thanks. It's also from the Christmas Market. I love this time of year and everything that goes with it. I'm Marian. I own this place. I haven't seen either of you here before. Here for a visit, or just passing through?'

'A visit,' Iris said. 'We're here for the weekend. I'm Iris and this is my best friend Elodie.'

'Very pleased to meet you.' Marian waved both hands and arms in the air as if to indicate Elodie and Iris could sit anywhere they wanted. 'As you can see, you can sit wherever you like. The torrential rain earlier seems to have kept everyone inside, but now the sun has come out, maybe the locals will too.'

'The rain's been replaced by a bitterly cold wind,' Elodie said.

'So maybe not then.' Marian shrugged. 'Ah well. They'll come out for lunch, no matter what the weather. At least I hope they will. There are menus on the tables, and one or two specials on the board over there.'

She pointed to a large blackboard covered with white swirly writing, offering delights such as maple syrup pancake crunch, Marian's mega breakfast, festive French toast, and clementine and cranberry Christmas muffins.

'Ooh! Christmas muffins for me, please,' Elodie said. 'And hot chocolate, if you have it.'

Marian gasped theatrically, placing one hand on her forehead and one on her chest.

'*If I have it*?' she repeated, in an equally dramatic voice before laughing in a way that made her sound as if she might be in pain, although she clearly wasn't. 'What sort of café would I be running if I didn't have hot chocolate, especially at this time of year? And not just hot chocolate. Festive hot chocolate. Delicious hot chocolate. And several varieties.' Her gaze darted towards the door and she gave a small laugh and winked. 'Speaking of delicious and hot. Here comes Archer.'

She hadn't lowered her voice as the café door opened, so the person coming in must have heard at least a part of what she had said but Marian didn't seem bothered.

A blast of artic-like air accompanied a tall, strapping man with broad shoulders, long legs, dark hair of the richest brown Elodie had ever seen and a smile warm enough to melt the biggest iceberg.

Jingle Bells rang out from the doormat as his large boot stepped on Father Christmas' face but Elodie was certain she also heard a choir of angels singing Hal-le-lu-jah! Or maybe she'd imagined that.

Every hair on her body stood to attention; at least it felt as if they had, and she knew her mouth was probably open; perhaps she was even drooling, although she hoped that wasn't the case.

The man had the looks of a movie star and hair to match. His faded jeans, quality walking boots and heavy-looking jacket gave him the air of a lumber jack and his height, frame, the way he held himself – and that smile, gave him the aura of a demi-god.

He glanced briefly at Iris and then at Elodie and did a sort of double take before furrowing his brows slightly and looking away towards Marian, with that gorgeous smile back in place.

'Morning, Archer. I hear it's cold out there. Want me to warm you up?' Marian's voice now had a seductive slant to it.

'Morning, Marian. Who wouldn't want that? But I'm saving all my treats till Christmas, so I'll just have one of your clementine and cranberry Christmas muffins for now, thanks.' He glanced at Elodie and Iris once again, this time with the sexiest grin Elodie had ever seen. 'I see I've caught the Christmas rush.'

'I think there's a cream for that,' Marian joked. 'Want me to rub it in for you?'

He gave a snort of laughter and shot a look at Marian. 'You're too kind. But no.' He then fixed his gaze on Elodie. 'Hello ladies. I hope I'm not pushing in.'

Marian started to make a crude remark but he raised one hand and said, 'Thank you, Marian.' She immediately stopped – although she laughed like a hyena drunk on Christmas sherry.

'Er ... Hello. And no,' Elodie said, looking from the man called Archer, to Marian and back again, wondering if they were an item, or merely good friends. The banter clearly wasn't unusual, judging by the way each of them reacted. 'We were just ordering.'

A slight frown creased Archer's forehead. 'Which means I am pushing in. Sorry. You go ahead. I can wait.'

Elodie had completely forgotten what she'd ordered but Iris reminded her by saying, 'I'll have the same as El. The muffin and a hot chocolate. What varieties did you say you've got?'

Marian winked at Archer. 'These lovely ladies are Elodie and Iris and they're here for the weekend. Not that you'd be the slightest bit interested, I know.'

He raised his brows, smiled and again, said, 'Hello.'

Before either Elodie or Iris could respond to that with anything other than a smile and a nod, Marian continued: 'I've got cinnamon hot chocolate, or mint, or cranberry, or rum and raisin – that's mainly rum but there is one chocolate-covered raisin floating on the top, just for good measure. There's also eggnog hot chocolate, brandy cream topped hot chocolate, and my own favourite, the melting snowman hot chocolate, which is hot chocolate covered in a sea of snowy cream, with a snowman made from mini marshmallows, clinging on to a log which is actually a chocolate flake.'

Elodie and Iris exchanged glances.

'We'll each have that one,' Iris said. 'And we'll sit at that table in the window.'

'Coming right up,' Marian smiled at them and then looked at Archer once more. 'Are you having hot chocolate too, Archer?'

'No thanks. But I will have one of your cappuccinos. Not the festive one. Just normal.'

'Remind me, Archer. Is your middle name Bah Humbug?'

'Yep. Archer Scrooge Bah Humbug Rhodes. That's me.'

Elodie couldn't help but glance in his direction as she and Iris made their way to the table and even once they sat down, she flicked a look at him, quickly casting her eyes down when she met his intense gaze.

'Stella was in yesterday,' Marian said to Archer, still grinning at him. 'She and Nosy Parker nearly came to blows.'

'That's hardly news,' Archer said.

'Stella thinks everyone should be invited to the Church Christmas Tree Lighting Ceremony tonight, including The Great Unwashed. You can imagine what old Nosy had to say about that. I kept out of it, of course.'

Archer laughed, and Elodie couldn't stop the sigh from escaping. His laugh was as infectious as Iris' smile. Unfortunately, it seemed he may have heard Elodie's sigh as he looked directly at her. But only for a moment. And then he returned his attention to Marian.

'Yeah, right. The day you keep out of anything will be the day the world ends. And you really shouldn't refer to the newcomers as The Great Unwashed, Marian. I know you use the term affectionately, but it's derogatory, nonetheless.'

Marian shrugged. 'Oh phooey. I can't help myself. You know me. Sorry, ladies. We're being rude. We're talking about some of our neighbours.'

'I'm sure these ladies aren't interested in our local goings on,' Archer said, sounding as if he wasn't that interested himself.

'Nonsense,' said Marian, putting the finishing touches to Elodie and Iris' hot chocolates and adding them to a tray along with two of her special muffins.

'Oh, we are,' Iris confirmed. 'At least I am.'

Marian stuck out her tongue at Archer who merely shook his head as she carried the tray to the table in the window and explained.

'Stella Pinkheart's a retired school teacher and a bit of a busy body. She and Nosy – oh, that's actually Rosie Parker, but we all call her Nosy Parker – because she is. Anyway, she and Stella are supposed to be great friends but they're as different as it's possible to be. And The Great Unwashed are the residents of the new housing estate. I know I shouldn't call them that, especially as most of them are really nice, but I do it with love. Nosy can't abide any of them which is pretty awkward, bearing in mind she's the vicar's sister. She was against the estate being built and she opposes anything and everything that any of those residents want to do. For the first time in the history of Clementine Cove, there's going to be a big Christmas tree beside the church and tonight's the Tree Lighting Ceremony for it. You should come along if you're free. Strictly speaking, it's by invitation only, but I've just invited you. Stella thinks everyone should be invited. Nosy disagrees.'

'Life is thrilling in Clementine Cove,' Archer said with a sardonic smile as he still waited patiently for his coffee and muffin.

Marian returned to her counter and prepared his order. 'Anyway, I simply pointed out that Christmas was a time for love and peace and harmony. A time when we should all come together.'

Archer raised his brows. 'Where did you hear that?'

Marian poured his coffee into a takeaway mug. 'On one of those cheesy Christmas adverts on TV the night before.'

'Perfect timing then.' He took the coffee and the bag in which she'd put a muffin, and paid her.

'Don't you want to know what Nosy said?'

'Not particularly. No. I think I can imagine. I'll see you tonight.'

'Yep. Me, Stella, Nosy ... and if Stella has her way, no doubt some of The Great Unwashed. There may be trouble.'

'Have a good day, Marian.' Archer smiled and turned to walk away, glancing briefly and nodding his head at Elodie and Iris. 'You too, ladies.' He opened the door and hesitated, glancing back over his shoulder. 'If you fancy something stronger during your stay, I own the village pub just over the way on Arrow Point. It's called The Bow and Quiver. And yes. I've heard all the jokes about Arrow Point, The Bow and Quiver, and my name. Anyway, just to prove I'm not a total Bah Humbug, or Grinch, or Scrooge, the first drink is on me. Hope to see you later.'

'Bloody Hell!' Marian said, as Archer quickly closed the door behind him. 'One of you has clearly made an impression. I don't think I've ever heard Archer offer a stranger a free drink. And I've known him all my life.'

Chapter 6

'That was weird,' Elodie said, twenty minutes later as she and Iris left the Cove Café and got into Iris' car to drive to the Millside shopping centre. 'One minute Marian was chatty and friendly and telling us all about the locals, the next she looked at us as if we were vampires at a blood bank.'

'Yeah. Right after she asked where we were staying and I said at my recently departed uncle's cottage.'

'And she clearly knew who you meant because she said – or should I say, screeched, "Clementine Cottage!" and immediately dashed off.'

'Even when I called out and asked to pay, she didn't seem keen to come out from her kitchen, did she? Or was I imagining that?'

Elodie shook her head. 'You weren't imagining it.'

Iris sighed as she turned on the ignition. 'I was going to ask her about Stanley and whether she liked him or not, but after that reaction, I thought it better not to.'

'I felt the same. And yet she'd been gossiping about people she obviously knows well, so why the sudden change? Unless she disliked your uncle as much as she seems to dislike Nosy – I mean, Rosie Parker, and she didn't want to talk about him in case she said something rude.'

'Like calling him something as awful as The Great Unwashed, you mean?' Iris smirked. 'It's not funny, I know, but I can almost hear Rosie saying that, can't you? In that rather upmarket voice of hers while looking down her nose. Beauty is clearly only skin deep as far as the vicar's sister is concerned.'

'I wonder if we should've said something to Marian about your uncle.' Elodie glanced back at the café. 'I mean, perhaps if we'd told her you'd never met the man and that your family didn't like him, we might have got a totally different reaction from her.'

'Well, I'm not going back to find out.' Iris laughed. 'We'll see her at the Church Christmas Tree Lighting Ceremony so we can say something to her tonight.'

'Are we going then?'

Iris raised her brows and threw Elodie a look of disbelief. 'Seriously, El? It's the Christmas Tree Lighting Ceremony. Of course we're going. Are you saying you don't want to?'

'What? No! As if I would say that. Although don't you think it's odd that the vicar and Rosie didn't invite us this morning? They seemed so keen to welcome us to the church.'

'Yeah. That was strange. Maybe they just forgot. The vicar did say he'd forgotten he hadn't left a key. Perhaps his memory's failing him, like he said it was.'

'Rosie's wasn't. She could've mentioned it.'

'Perhaps she decided to include us amongst The Great Unwashed.'

Elodie laughed. 'Then won't she get a surprise when we turn up tonight?'

'Exactly. And you can drool over Archer ... whatever his name was, even more.'

Elodie gasped before running her fingers around the cuff of her coat sleeve as Iris laughed louder.

'I have no idea what you could possibly mean by that. And his name is Archer Rhodes. Not that I'm in the least bit interested.'

'Was that a flying pig I just saw, or a flying reindeer? Not interested! I'm surprised you could get your tongue back off the floor.'

Elodie scrunched up her face. 'Was it that obvious?'

Iris shrugged. 'To me, yes. But maybe not to him or Marian. I think she might've teased you about it if she'd noticed you'd as good as fallen in love with the guy at first sight.'

'In love? Who said anything about love? In lust, maybe. Probably. Definitely. But love? No. Although ... I think it's possible that I could fall in love with a man like that. Couldn't you?'

Iris thought about that for a moment or two, before shaking her head.

'I don't think so. He was handsome, I'll give him that. And he had a gorgeous smile. His voice was pleasant too. Sort of soft and sultry and yet somehow deep and masterful. And he looked as if he had a good body if his face and neck and legs were anything to judge by. Plus, he didn't really want to gossip but he let Marian have her say. And he genuinely seemed to like her in spite of the fact she's possibly a bit bitchy. Not forgetting he offered us a free drink.'

'Sounds like you're already more in love with him than I could be!' Elodie interjected.

'Nope. He's dark-haired, and that's a deal breaker for me. You know I like my men blond and beautiful. Not dark and swarthy-looking. That's your type.'

'My type? I don't have a type. And certainly not swarthy-looking. If I did have a type, it would be professional and intelligent looking.'

'Professional and intelligent? Since when?' Iris laughed. 'You do have a type. And it's swarthy. The outdoorsy type. Rubin for one. And, the four or five others before him. Plus, of course, that bastard, Ben. Sorry. I know I shouldn't have mentioned him. But almost every guy you've ever dated has had dark hair. Maybe that's your mistake. Try dating a blond-haired guy. He might be The One.' She sighed loudly. 'But I can see you're already half in love with Archer Rhodes and I suspect we'll be spending quite a lot of this weekend in The Bow and Quiver. It's a good thing I'm not tee-total. Now, am I going insane, or is this shopping centre harder to get into than Fort Knox? Where the hell is the turn off for it?'

'Er ... I think we just drove past it.'

Iris tutted. 'Why didn't you say something?'

'Sorry. I was too busy thinking about what you were saying. I hate to admit it but maybe you're right. Most of the men in my past are dark-haired. Perhaps it's time I started dating a different type of man.'

'I was joking, El. Hair and skin colour don't dictate a man's – or a woman's, character. And that's what's important. Not the way they look. It's merely a coincidence that all the guys you've dated have been dark-haired.'

'Is it? I don't know now. You've got me thinking.'

'There's a first time for everything.'

'Funny. And for someone who has just driven past the turn off to the shopping centre again, I'd say that's a bit rich.'

'Bugger!' Iris said, circling Moneymaker Circle for the third time that morning.

Elodie continued, 'But it's as good a place as any to start. We're thirty-five, Iris, and we're both still single. I know it shouldn't bother us. And most of the time it doesn't bother me. But Christmas always makes me think about how good it would be to have someone special in my life.'

'You've got someone special in your life.'

Elodie laughed. 'I mean someone other than you, you idiot. And my family. Er ... you've just driven past the turn off again. What is wrong with you? It's the biggest road off this roundabout! Pound Road.'

Which meant Iris drove around Moneymaker Circle yet again but this time she crawled at a snail's pace to ensure she didn't miss the turn off for the road leading to Millside shopping centre.

Once parked, they were surprised to see the Christmas Market occupied both the ground and upper floors of the centre, with small log cabins covered in fake snow and strung with myriad fairy lights positioned opposite the main shops and dotted all around the escalators and walkways.

Mingling with the crowds of Christmas shoppers, they discovered the cabins sold handcrafted goods of every description, including candles and decorated lanterns, Christmas ornaments, cushions, throws, Christmas stockings, wrapping paper and mini Christmas trees made from a variety of materials.

There were cabins selling festive dog and cat treats, and several selling tempting titbits for human consumption, including mince pies, Christmas cakes, chocolate logs and stollen.

The cabins selling eggnog, hot spiced cider, buttered rum, mulled wine and its German equivalent, gluhwein, and schnapps seemed particularly popular. More so than those selling tea, coffee and even hot chocolate.

The heady aromas filled the air and mingled with the scent of pine, but in some places, the tempting smell of hot sausage rolls, festive beef burgers, ham burgers and even pizza was almost overpowering, drawing people to them in droves.

Other cabins offered wooden toys for sale, and knitted and crocheted animals and dolls. There were cabins selling gloves and scarves and hats. Cabins selling Christmas crackers and party games.

Elodie and Iris spent a lot of time – and money at the cabins selling bath and shower products, and Iris bought out nearly all the stock of Christmas earrings from one cabin. That definitely made that seller's Christmas.

The cacophony of chattering voices, laughter, children screaming, some for joy, others for something they wanted and were told they couldn't have, was deafening. Added to that, Christmas carols rang out from speakers all around the centre, and people dressed as elves walked around and wished everyone a very Merry Christmas while handing out leaflets with details of the timings for 'Photos with Santa in his grotto', the queue for which already snaked like multi-coloured tinsel, halfway around the ground floor.

Elodie and Iris had only intended to spend an hour at the Christmas Market but they stayed and had a Christmas lunch at one of the cafés so it was almost 2 p.m. by the time they returned to Clementine Cottage.

When they stepped inside, Iris picked up an envelope from the doormat and she grinned at Elodie once she'd opened it.

'What is it?' Elodie asked, taking off her coat and hanging it on the rack beside the door.

'It's a Royal invitation.' Iris held up the crisp white card edged in gold. 'Well, an invite from the Parkers to 'cocktails and canapés at Rosehip Cottage, followed by the Christmas Tree Lighting Ceremony at St Mary's in the Wood church.' So it seems we're not considered members of The Great Unwashed, after all.'

Elodie laughed. 'I feel oddly relieved by that.' Until realisation dawned. 'Er ... I didn't bring anything suitable to wear to a cocktail party. Did you?'

Iris' mouth dropped open. 'Nope. I thought we'd spend most of the time here, seeing what the place was like and maybe have a look around the village and go out for a drink and possibly dinner, but I just brought smart trousers and jumpers for that.'

'Me too.' After a moment, Elodie grinned. 'Are you thinking what I'm thinking?'

Iris sighed and nodded as Elodie put her coat back on.

'We're going to have to head back to that damn roundabout again and go clothes shopping at Millside.'

By the time they'd both purchased dresses they deemed suitable for a cocktail party and the tree lighting, it was late afternoon.

They parked the car and walked down the path towards the cottage but stopped in their tracks as they took in the vista before them.

The sun was setting over the bay, casting ribbons of crimson, purple, blue and pale gold across the sky above a carpet-like silver sea. They stood huddled together against the cold and watched the sun disappear below the horizon.

Elodie noticed something out of the corner of her eye and when she turned her head she saw the two foxes and the robin they'd seen earlier. She gently nudged Iris and whispered, 'We've got company.'

Iris sucked in a breath and smiled. 'Oh wow! Twice in one day. That's incredible.'

After a moment or two Elodie asked, 'Do you think this is normal? I mean, do foxes and robins just nip in and out of cottage gardens in places like this? Or do you think that, maybe, your uncle fed them, and that's why they've appeared twice, shortly after we've parked? As if they know someone's at the cottage. I didn't see a bird feeder or anything, or any bowls for the foxes, but perhaps they've been cleared away.'

Iris met her look. 'I've no idea. It's possible, I suppose. Should we put some food out for them, just in case? Or maybe we should wait and ask Rosie or the vicar tonight. We're only here for the weekend, after all. If Stanley wasn't feeding them, we don't want to start and then leave.'

'You're right. We'll ask tonight.'

It was as if the creatures understood because just a second or two later the robin flew away and the foxes scampered off into the trees in exactly the same direction they'd gone earlier.

'I'm definitely falling in love with this place,' Elodie said.

'Me too,' Iris agreed.

'But now I think I need a thirty-minute nap before we get showered and dolled up for the Parker's little do.'

'Me too,' said Iris again, as they headed towards the front door.

Chapter 7

Elodie offered to drive to Rosehip Cottage. It was too far for them to walk in the cold and dark, especially as they didn't know the area, and it seemed to be surprisingly dark in the countryside. Much darker than either of them expected. There were a few streetlights dotted here and there, but none near Clementine Cottage and certainly not across the fields leading to the church.

Even the bright lights from the nearby 'new' housing estate were blocked out by the barrier of trees edging the cottage garden, many of which were evergreens, and some of which were thick, dense holly bushes and trees, each overflowing with an abundance of red berries, still waiting to be feasted on by the birds.

Rosie and the vicar had said it was only five minutes' walk away across the fields, and the sun had been shining for most of the day, but from what they had seen earlier, everything still looked too muddy from the downpour that morning

Elodie was tired from the party the previous night and had decided not to drink this evening, partly to give her liver a rest and partly because she was concerned that she might fall asleep if she had even one glass of wine. The nap had refreshed her, but not enough to give her stamina for a drinking session.

Not that the likes of Rosie and the vicar would probably entertain such a thing. Elodie was fairly sure they wouldn't. Guests would no doubt be served a couple of cocktails, if they were lucky, and just enough posh nosh to feed the friendly robin.

The invitation stated 7 p.m. but Elodie and Iris were late. Fashionably late, Elodie hoped, but the expression on Rosie's immaculately made-up face when they were shown into the drawing room of Rosehip Cottage by a smartly dressed butler, informed them otherwise. Rosie was clearly not amused.

'Sorry,' Elodie said, a little intimidated by the fact the Parkers had a butler, even one hired specifically for this occasion, and also by the fact that all eyes in the somewhat cramped drawing room, turned to see who had had the audacity to be tardy to one of

Rosie Parker's exclusive soirées. 'We got lost.'

'Lost?' Rosie queried, from her prime position in the centre of the room, as if that was impossible.

'Yeah,' Iris confirmed. 'We've driven around that damn Moneymaker Circle so many times today we should be rich by now.'

Only one person laughed at that, and Elodie couldn't help but smile. Archer Rhodes clearly had a sense of humour similar to her and her best friend. She met his eyes across the room and he nodded a hello as Rosie glared from Elodie and Iris to Archer and back again.

'Why were you at Moneymaker Circle?' Rosie queried, but didn't wait for a reply. 'It doesn't matter. You're here now. Let me get you a cocktail.'

She clicked her fingers and a waitress appeared, bearing a silver tray on which two glasses stood.

'Were these reserved for us?' Elodie whispered to Iris.

'I think you mean rationed,' Iris quipped, raising one eyebrow.

'As I was saying,' Rosie said, sending a look filled with daggers of ice in Elodie and Iris' direction.

She had clearly been interrupted in the middle of a speech. No wonder she'd given them that icy stare.

But before she had a chance to continue, a woman with an even posher voice than Rosie's said, 'Daaahrling! Aren't you going to introduce us to your new *friends*?'

Now Rosie looked mortified.

'Oh! My dear Cordelia! How remiss of me. I assumed you'd already met. But please, let me introduce you.' She waved her hand and the crowd of people around her parted like the Red Sea, allowing the other woman a clear line of sight to Elodie and Iris. 'This is Iris Talbot and her best friend, Elodie ... I didn't catch the surname.'

'Abbott,' Elodie said, wishing she hadn't as everyone appeared to be staring at her and Iris as if they actually hadn't washed and they smelled of something unpleasant.

Rosie continued, 'They're spending the weekend at Clementine Cottage. Iris is dear Stanley Talbot's niece. Surely you knew?'

It was obvious this Cordelia woman hadn't a clue – and why should she? But her reaction was surprising, to say the least. She let slip a tiny but audible gasp, and an expensively manicured hand shot to her throat as if something were suddenly strangling her.

And, as if the curious stares weren't bad enough, she wasn't the only person to gasp, or look astonished – and not in a good way, or to mutter something to the person beside them.

But Rosie's expression was one of triumphant one-upmanship.

Elodie was drawn to look at Archer and she got the shock of her life.

The colour had drained from his face, his eyes were narrow slits, his generous lips were bereft of even a hint of a smile and instead were a tight, hard line and his brow twitched as if he had a nervous affliction. He emptied his glass in one swig, placed it unceremoniously on the mantlepiece nearby and turned and marched towards the door.

Elodie couldn't help herself. Without thinking, she reached out her hand and caught his arm as he strode past, her fingers not even making an impression on the muscular biceps beneath his black jacket.

'What's wrong?' she asked.

She met his eyes and saw something akin to distaste, mingled with regret.

'Everything,' he said, through almost gritted teeth. 'Excuse me.'

He glared at her hand as if she held him in a burning vice and she hurriedly but reluctantly removed it.

'I don't understand,' she pleaded.

'I wish I didn't,' was all he said, before hurrying away.

She looked at Iris who seemed equally confused.

'I don't know about The Great Unwashed, I feel like we've got leprosy or something,' Iris whispered, and a moment later, when the Reverend Wilfred Parker approached them with an awkward smile she asked him, 'Why is everyone staring at us like that?'

'Ah,' he said, in a soft and soothing tone. 'Perhaps we should have mentioned this. Not everyone in Clementine Cove ... liked your uncle, shall we say. In fact, one or two, positively *disliked* him. But it's most unchristian-like of them to tar you with the same brush, and I shall make that point during my sermon this Sunday.'

'Thanks,' Iris said. 'That's helpful. We'll be leaving on Sunday.'

Her sarcasm was completely lost on him because his smile widened.

'Don't mention it, my dear. Anything we can do to make you feel welcome in our village is well worth the effort. Why don't you come and chat with some of our other guests and let them see that, you may be Stanley's niece, but the similarity ends there. Assuming it does, of course. Come along.'

He clearly expected them to follow him but before they did, Iris said, '"Well worth the effort"? That sounded pretty unchristian-like of him!'

But Elodie was still picturing Archer's face and although some of the other guests made polite conversation, everyone she and Iris spoke to, seemed to be picking their words carefully.

Happily, Marian appeared to have mellowed since that morning and she chatted with them about the Christmas Market, telling Iris how much she loved the new Christmas stocking earrings Iris was wearing.

But when Elodie tried to bring up the subject of Archer and his reaction to the news about Iris' uncle, she clamped up again, pointed to a woman with pink hair and said, 'Ah. There's Stella. I need to have a word with her.' And she disappeared into a corner with the pink-haired woman who was obviously Stella Pinkheart.

Thankfully, the cocktail and canapés didn't last long. Iris had been right. Everything did seem to be rationed. At least it felt like that.

'Will everyone follow me?' Rosie Parker said, in a tone that made it a command rather than a request.

She led them all outside and across the lane to the church, beside which stood a massive and impressive Christmas tree and despite the fact that the tree could be seen from almost anywhere in the village, everyone oohed and ahhed as if a large cover had been removed and the tree had been revealed in all its glory.

The Reverend gave a speech, which sounded a lot like a sermon, about how Christmas was a time for forgiveness and for coming together; for seeing the good in those around us and not merely the bad. For accepting people for who they are, not assuming they were motivated by the same things that their family or friends or relatives might be.

He said a lot more besides, but Elodie zoned him out and instead stared across the mouth of the bay towards the lights of The Bow and Quiver – the pub owned by Archer Rhodes.

Archer hadn't come to the tree lighting, having walked out earlier and she couldn't help but wonder why. Why had he reacted in the way he had? No one else had walked out, as far as Elodie had seen. It was all rather odd ... and extremely confusing.

Was he in his pub, looking across the bay at the tree through one of those welcoming-looking windows?

The sudden burst of cheers and clapping made Elodie jump and only then did she see that the tree lights were on. They twinkled and sparkled in the cold night air giving a warming glow and somehow a flicker of hope.

But an eerie mist swept in from the sea, swirling around the tree like microscopic demons, bringing with it a waft of even colder air. Elodie shivered and tugged her coat tighter around her, glancing at Iris who was staring at the tree, deep in thought.

'Penny for them,' Elodie said, giving Iris a playful nudge.

'What? Oh. I was just wishing that I knew what had caused the rift between my uncle and my mum and dad. And wondering what my uncle could've said or done to make so many people here dislike him.'

Chapter 8

The first thing Elodie did the moment she and Iris returned to Clementine Cottage shortly after 9 p.m. was to search for the largest glasses she could find in the display cabinet in the dining room. They were actually gin glasses not wine, but she didn't care and she knew Iris wouldn't either. They had brought six bottles of their favourite red wine with them and each glass held exactly half a bottle.

'I need this,' Elodie said, as she and Iris clinked the glasses.

'You're not alone there,' Iris said. 'I thought Christmas tree lightings and cocktail parties were supposed to be fun. I've had better times putting out the rubbish after Christmas Day lunch.'

That was literally true. Iris had once met one of her boyfriends whilst taking out a black sack on a particularly icy Christmas Day. She had slipped on the black ice on the path of her parents' house and skidded slap bang into a handsome blond-haired hunk who was taking his dog out for a walk. The man broke her fall, they dated for several months, and ultimately, Iris broke his heart. At least that was the way her parents told the story. Iris said they had simply taken several months to discover they wanted different things from life.

'It didn't feel very festive either, did it?' Elodie said. 'Even before the persona non grata incident. Or I suppose that should be personae non gratae, as neither of us seemed very welcome.'

And the second thing she did was persuade Iris to phone Frank and Sharon and ask them about the rift between them and Stanley.

'If you tell them what happened here tonight, and also about Marian's reaction in the café this morning, I'm sure they'll tell you something.'

She was right. Frank and Sharon, who were sipping early evening cocktails on the Lido deck of the ship, at one of the many outside bars when Iris called, were horrified to hear their only daughter had been made to feel like some sort of outcast.

'I need to know what caused the rift, Dad,' Iris said.

'We'll return to our suite and call you back from there,' Frank said, and when he and Sharon did, Iris put them on speakerphone so that Elodie could hear.

'Stanley wasn't a nice man,' Frank said. 'He wasn't even a nice kid. He was always getting into trouble when we were young, but more often than not he usually managed to find a way to get out of it, scot-free. He was cute and charming as a kid, and handsome and debonair as a young man, but good looks and smooth talking didn't always work, he told me, so he realised early on that he had to find another way. I still remember what he told me that day. "Knowledge is power, Frank. Everyone's got something they would rather someone didn't find out. It may be something small. It may be something big. But it's there. You just have to know how to find out what it is – and how and when to use it to your advantage." I couldn't believe what he was telling me. Until later.'

'And that's why you cast him out of your lives?' Iris asked. 'I don't understand.'

'No. We cast him out because ... he found out something about your mother that he thought I didn't know, and he tried to use that to extort some money from her. His plan backfired though. For two reasons. One. Because Sharon had already told me, and two, because neither your mum nor I would ever condone such appalling not to mention, criminal behaviour.'

Iris gasped. 'What ... what was it that he knew about Mum? It must've been something bad if he thought he could blackmail her!'

Sharon sighed loudly. Frank also had the phone on speaker.

'Oh darling, it was so long ago. And these days, it probably wouldn't seem much at all. But I suppose it's something you should know. Before I met your father, I had a child.'

Iris nearly dropped the phone and Elodie stifled a gasp.

'You what!' Iris screeched. 'Are you telling me that somewhere out there I have a sibling?'

'No, darling. Sadly not. Which is why we haven't told you about this. I was very young. Only sixteen and I thought I was in love. When I discovered I was going to have a baby, the father did a runner. My parents decided I should have my baby and they would help me raise him. He ... he died in my arms when he was just three days old. He had a congenital heart defect and there was nothing the hospital could do to save him. Many babies born with that are lucky and survive, often into adulthood and beyond. Unfortunately, he didn't. I named him Francis, after my grandfather and losing him broke my heart. I still don't know how Stanley found out, but he did. Luckily, I had already told your father all about my baby, but your paternal grandparents weren't ... overjoyed when they found out. And yes. Your uncle Stanley told them. They tried to persuade Frank not to marry me, but he wouldn't listen. You don't know this either, but we may as well tell you it all now. They refused to come to our wedding, and they didn't speak to us for almost five years. It was only when you were born that they saw the error of their ways and we were able to mend the bridges. But we flatly refused to ever have anything to do with Stanley.'

'Bloody hell, Mum! I can't believe it. What else have you been keeping from me?'

'Nothing, darling. I promise you.'

Elodie got up, leaving Iris and her parents to chat, mouthing, 'I'll give you some privacy. I'll be in the kitchen when you're done.'

Ten minutes later, Iris joined her and opened a second bottle of wine.

'Wow'! she said. 'Can you believe that? I had absolutely no idea.'

Elodie shook her head and reached out and squeezed Iris' hand.

'Are you okay?'

Iris nodded and looked Elodie directly in the eye. 'It was a shock. I can't deny that. But yeah. I'm fine. Mum says that even after all these years, she still finds it hard to talk about the son she lost. She said she still grieves for him, and Dad knows she does and gives her the time and space to do so, or cuddles and understanding when she needs them, but she prefers to grieve for him alone. That's why she never told me. She said she didn't want me to feel upset over someone I had never met or known existed, so she decided it was better not to tell me about him. And she's right. Now I sort of feel as if I've lost a brother. Well, a half-brother. But I haven't. Not really. Because he died long before I was born, and he wasn't part of our family. Of me and Mum and Dad. Even so, we're going to talk more when they get back. But … I think I owe you an apology.'

'Me? What for?'

'For not telling you about my uncle Stanley. I couldn't understand why you were upset about it. But now I can. Now I know how you felt when you discovered I'd kept a secret from you. I should've realised after that bastard, Ben's bombshell because although he was your boyfriend and you were devastated, I was upset about that too because of how it affected you. But now I know first-hand what it feels like to discover you haven't been told something you feel, in some way, you should have. I'm really sorry,

El. And I'm sorry for bringing up Ben again. What is wrong with me?'

Iris sighed and shook her head, giving Elodie an apologetic smile. Elodie gave her a hug.

'That's okay. But let's make a pact. There will never be secrets between us again. Ever. No matter how small or insignificant we think they may be.'

'I'll drink to that,' Iris said, and they clinked glasses to seal the deal.

Chapter 9

'I've just had an awful thought,' Elodie said, a few minutes later as they returned to the sitting room to make a fire. They'd been discussing Sharon's revelation while making cheese on toast and then sitting at the kitchen table, finishing off the second bottle of wine and devouring their supper. Now they planned to put up some decorations that they'd bought at the Christmas Market to make the cottage more festive and to sit in front of the fire, once it was made, for an hour or two to get into the Christmas spirit after the let down of the tree lighting. 'What if your uncle was doing that here?'

'What? Blackmailing people?'

Iris dropped onto one of the armchairs near the empty hearth and Elodie sat in the chair opposite.

'Yes. Don't look so dismissive. He told your dad that knowledge was power and he admitted he used that knowledge to his advantage. He tried to blackmail your mum, and she was his own brother's girlfriend. If he'd do that to his own family, who knows what he might do to ... other people. And it would explain the bizarre reaction we got this evening, wouldn't it? Plus, he's got that study, that laptop and all those filing cabinets but we still don't know what he did for a living. Maybe those filing cabinets don't contain the usual office paperwork. Maybe they contain something else entirely.'

'Bloody hell.' Iris sat bolt upright. 'You may be right. Let's go and see.'

They dashed to Stanley's office, their plans for decorating and a cosy night by the fire, forgotten, but all the drawers in the cabinets were locked.

'Do any of those keys the vicar gave you open them?'

Iris got the keys and tried each one in turn but none of them fitted the locks.

'They must be somewhere,' Iris said. 'The police bagged up everything Stanley had on him when they found him, and Arthur told Dad that when they contacted him, he'd asked them to give the keys to Reverend Parker, because, as the vicar said to us, it made sense for someone local to have the keys in case of an emergency and Arthur knew and trusted Wilfred Parker.'

They exchanged anxious glances.

'You don't think ...?'

'The vicar kept the keys to the cabinets?' Iris finished Elodie question. 'No. I can't see that somehow. And again, why would he? He's had them for a couple of days so that gave him plenty of time to come here and take anything he wanted. If he were that way inclined. Which, as a man of the cloth, he shouldn't be.'

'But he might. And maybe he's emptied the cabinets, or at least taken something from them.'

Iris gave her a look. 'Really? If he'd done that there would be no need for him to keep the keys and they'd be with this bunch.'

'I suppose so. Then where are they?'

Iris shrugged. 'No idea. But they must be somewhere, mustn't they? Unless someone else took them.' She shook her head. 'No. I think we're dipping our toes into fantasy land now. The keys are here. I'm sure of it. We just need to find out where they are. I can't see any key racks. Maybe they're in one of the drawers in his desk.' She rolled her eyes. 'That makes much more sense. We should've thought of that before getting all murder mystery-ish.'

But the keys weren't in the desk drawers and even one of those was locked.

'This is getting ridiculous,' Iris said, trying all the keys again to see if one fitted the drawer of the desk. But none did.

They searched all the shelves and bookcases, and went into the hall to look for a key rack there and then into the kitchen before returning to the study.

'They'd be in this room,' Elodie said. 'You wouldn't want to have to get up and go elsewhere to get them, would you? It doesn't make sense.'

'I'm with you on that. The keys must be in here. But where?'

After another, more extensive search, Elodie had a hunch. When she moved the framed photograph of the two foxes and the robin that was hanging on the wall beside Stanley's desk, she found, taped to the back of it, two sets of keys in a little match-sized box. One set was for the desk and the other was for the cabinets, judging by the shape and size of them.

'Why would he hide them there?' Iris asked.

This time Elodie shrugged. 'No idea. But something drew me to that photo.'

'Spooky!' Iris laughed.

'Intuition,' Elodie said. 'Plus it's right by his desk.'

'Pity he hadn't also taped a piece of paper there with the laptop password written on it.'

'He must've memorised that. I think we may as well forget about the laptop. Come on then. Open them!'

Opening the cabinets, they found rows of coloured files and each one had a person's name written on the tab clipped to the top of that individual folder. Some were thicker than the others and they seemed to be in alphabetical order, but then some were batched together with other files of the same colour, breaking the alphabetical sequence, but starting again in that particular colour. So the first drawer of grey files went from A-D and then the next drawer from E but then a batch of blue files went from A-Z and the drawer below that contained more grey files and went from F-H.

'I'm not sure I follow his system,' Iris said.

'Nor me.' Elodie frowned. 'It doesn't make sense. Why not just put them all in alphabetical order based on the colour of the folder? So grey A-Z then blue A-Z then pink A-Z and so on.'

'That's what I'd do.' Iris nodded her agreement. 'Let's look for a name we know. Let's start with the Parkers.'

'Or Marian Blythe. That begins with a B.'

'No! Really?' Iris laughed. 'I did go to school, you know. I even got a gold star for my ABCs when we were six, if you recall.'

Elodie tutted. 'I do, as it happens. What I meant was B comes before P. And yes, I realise you know that too. What I'm saying is that the Bs are right here. We're not sure which drawer the Ps are in.'

'Aren't peas usually in pods? Or in bags in the freezer,' Iris joked.

'You should be on the stage.' Elodie gave her a playful shove.

'Okay,' Iris said. 'Bs it is.'

It didn't take them too long to spot the folder with Marian's name written on the tab, but it wasn't in the Bs in the first drawer of grey files. It was in the second drawer amongst the batch of blue ones. And it was one of the thickest of the blues. And just behind that, a few letters back, they saw Stella Pinkheart's name.

'Perhaps the colours relate to how friendly he was with each person. Or how well he knew them,' Elodie said.

'Or how much info he had on them,' added Iris.

Elodie shook her head. 'No. That can't be the case because Marian's and Stella's files are both blue but Marian's is much thicker than Stella's.

'You're right.' Iris suddenly grabbed Elodie's arm. 'Maybe the colours relate to how useful or how valuable to Stanley that info might be.' Her eyes were bright and filled with excitement as if she'd just cracked a secret code. Which in a way she might have done.

'Yes. That makes more sense.'

'Now I've got to look for Rosie's and the vicar's. I've got to know what colours their files are.'

'Assuming he has files on them, of course.'

'Oh, El. Judging by the number of cabinets and drawers, I'd say it's a good bet that he's got files on everyone in this village. Possibly even further afield.'

'Everyone?' Elodie had been thinking it but she wasn't sure she wanted to know. 'Even Archer Rhodes?'

Iris shrugged, making the red noses on the reindeer earrings she'd worn to the cocktail party and tree lighting, glow brighter in the light.

'I think it's safe to assume the answer to that is yes. But we can look and then we'll know.'

They opened each drawer in turn until they found the files on Rosie and Wilfred. They were different colours, Rosie's being orange and Wilfred's being pink. They were also different thicknesses. Rosie's was thicker than Wilfred's.

And then they searched for Archer's folder and a massive knot formed in Elodie's stomach the moment they found it.

'What's wrong?' Iris questioned. 'You don't seem as excited as before.'

Elodie bit her lower lip before letting out a sigh.

'I'm not sure I want to do this. I don't like secrets, we both know that, but this feels ... wrong somehow. It feels as if we may be about to read all these people's personal diaries or something like that. You know? We don't know what these files contain but from what we do know, Stanley wasn't a nice man so these files probably don't contain anything ... good about any of these people. I'd really hate to think that someone could read a file containing things about me.'

'I get that. I wouldn't want anyone to read things about me either. But the thing is, El. If we don't look, we won't know what Stanley was up to and we won't know why people reacted to us the way they did when they discovered I was his niece. I think we need to read one or two just to find out. And besides. Don't you want to know more about Archer Rhodes? It was two years before you discovered that you weren't Ben's only girlfriend. That he had another one he'd dated for almost as long as you and that he had proposed to her too. If Archer is hiding something bad, wouldn't it be better to find out now before you risk getting hurt?'

'Firstly, Iris,' Elodie snapped. 'Will you please stop mentioning Ben!'

Iris scrunched up her face. 'Sorry. Sorry. Sorry. I'll never mention Ben again. Apart from just then. But that's it. Okay?'

She gave Elodie a puppy dog look and one of her smiles and Elodie smiled back.

'Okay. Thanks. Secondly, we're only here for a long weekend and after we leave on Sunday it's unlikely I'll ever be here again. So nothing's going to happen between me and Archer Rhodes. Other than, perhaps, a quick fling. Which I would love because it feels like forever since I had sex and it's Christmas and ... well anyway. It doesn't matter if Archer's bad or good because after this weekend, I'll never see him again.'

'Bad or good?' Iris burst out laughing. 'This isn't about Santa's naughty or nice list. Or maybe it is, in a way. Except Stanley was no Santa!'

'I think we can agree on that.'

'El?' Iris was suddenly serious. 'Is your not wanting to know what's in these files due to the fact that Archer's folder is red? And there are only two other red files apart from his. I think we're both assuming that grey is boring, yellow is slightly interesting, blue is more interesting, pink even more, orange much more and red much, much more ... as in ... the biggest secret ... and probably ... the worst.'

Elodie met her look and nodded.

'Partly. Yes. I think it is. He ... Archer that is ... looked really nice. The sort of guy you could trust. And yes I know we only met him briefly and we didn't really speak to him or anything but ... Oh, I don't know. All I can say is I had the strangest feeling when I saw him. Sort of like ... he was someone I could really fall for. Someone I could ...'

'Have great sex with.'

Elodie tutted. 'Yes. He definitely oozed sex appeal. But it was more than that. I felt ... I don't know. I was in love with Ben and look how that turned out.'

'I thought we weren't mentioning Ben. Sorry. But you can't compare what you've just said you felt about Archer with how you felt about ... that other guy whose name I won't be saying. It took you a while to fall for B ... him. You didn't even like him when you first met him. He charmed his way into your life and your heart.'

That was true. And he'd done a thorough job of it. Elodie still compared every man she dated to Ben – even though the man was a complete and utter bastard. He'd got her totally convinced he was the perfect guy. But it was all an illusion. The problem was, Elodie still held that image in her mind as the ideal man.

'He certainly did,' Elodie said.

'So what are you saying then? About these files, I mean. Are we going to read them or aren't we? Wait. Don't answer that. I don't think we should make a decision tonight. I think we should sleep on it and see how we feel in the morning. Agreed?'

Elodie glanced at the thick red folder with Archer Rhodes written on the tab and the knot in her stomach grew tighter.

Part of her wanted to grab it and read it from cover to cover and part of her wanted to pretend she hadn't seen the folder and that it wasn't red.

Another part of her wished she hadn't laid eyes on Archer Rhodes at all, because in spite of what she'd said about never seeing him again after this weekend, an even bigger part of her told her that was something she couldn't bear.

She'd seen the man only twice and for probably a maximum of fifteen minutes each time. They had exchanged merely a handful of words and yet she had the strangest feeling that Archer Rhodes was going to play an important part in her life this Christmas, even if she had no idea how that could possibly be so.

'Agreed,' she said, smiling wanly at Iris.

Iris closed the drawers and locked them, returning the keys to the back of the photo where they'd found them.

'Well,' she said, with an expression somewhere between horror and amusement on her face. 'It seems likely that everyone in Clementine Cove appears to have a secret – and Stanley knew them all. Now at least we can safely say that it doesn't take a genius to work out why Uncle Stanley wasn't popular. He's clearly been keeping more than a close eye on all the villagers. I said earlier that we could see half, if not all the village from various rooms in this cottage, so I think we know what all those window seats were for.'

'A place for your uncle to sit and watch the world go by. Literally. And then make notes of what the world did and who it did it with, perhaps?'

'Exactly.'

Elodie tried to stifle a yawn but failed. It was almost midnight and she was shattered. She hadn't had more than thirty minutes sleep the previous night and she needed to go to bed.

'Do you mind if I go to bed? I'm not sure I can stay awake much longer.'

'No. You go. I'll be right behind you. I just want to check all the doors are locked. I know Rosie said that Marian was probably wrong about someone sneaking around, but now that we've seen all these files, I wouldn't be surprised. Better to be safe than sorry.'

'Are you serious? Oh my God, Iris. Please don't say things like that.'

'Sorry. I was joking.'

'Fine. But it wasn't funny. Don't look at me like that.' Elodie gave in to Iris' smile and smiled back. 'Oh all right. Want a hand?'

'No thanks. It shouldn't take me too long.'

'Okay. Good night and pleasant dreams. See you in the morning.'

But Elodie only got as far as her bedroom door before she heard a piercing scream.

Chapter 10

'Iris! I'm coming!'

Elodie almost tumbled down the stairs in her haste and had to grab hold of the banister to prevent her from falling.

'Elodie! Was that you?'

Iris appeared at the foot of the staircase, her face ashen and taut with fear.

'What happened?' Elodie shrieked. 'Are you okay?'

Now Iris looked confused.

'I'm fine. You?'

Elodie furrowed her brows, staring at her friend.

'I'm fine. *You screamed.*'

'No. *You* screamed ... didn't you?'

'No. You–'

They both squealed when they heard the shrill cry once again.

'It's coming from outside,' Iris said, fear still etched on her face as they hugged one another close. A few moments later, she relaxed visibly and let out a sigh. 'I know what it is. Phew.' She placed a hand on her chest and her other hand on Elodie's arm. 'We're fine. It's those foxes we saw earlier. The vixen, I expect. I remember hearing it once, years ago when we stayed on a farm in the middle of the countryside. I nearly died of fright, but the farmer told us it was just a vixen's call. It's worse in late winter and the spring when it's mating season, but they do call out at other times throughout the year, or so he told us.'

'That was a fox? Seriously? I love foxes but I've never heard one do that. Then again, I haven't actually seen that many other than on TV. I thought someone had broken in and was trying to murder you!'

Iris laughed. 'Finding those files has set your imagination running wild, hasn't it?'

Elodie pulled a face. 'A bit, if I'm honest. Look.' She raised one hand in front of her. 'I'm still shaking. Have we got anything stronger than wine? I think I need a brandy or something.'

Iris shook her head. 'I just brought wine as we agreed. But maybe Stanley had brandy. I'll go and look.'

'I'm coming with you,' Elodie said, linking arms with Iris. 'This place looked cute and cosy before but now it's giving me the creeps.'

With most of the lights switched off, shadows seemed to lurk in every corner and although Elodie knew only she and Iris were in the cottage, a chill ran through her making her shiver.

Iris was right about those files playing with Elodie's imagination. Even as she'd been walking upstairs to bed she'd been wondering if Marian had really seen someone skulking around the cottage, and for some reason images of Archer Rhodes dressed from head to toe in black and looking extremely menacing, popped into her head.

She'd dismissed them immediately and told herself she was being ridiculous.

But then she'd heard that scream.

And for one terrible moment, she thought Archer Rhodes had broken in and was trying to steal that thick red folder with his name written on the tab.

Chapter 11

Elodie wasn't sure it had been a good thing that Stanley had indeed had something stronger than wine because now her head was thumping and the shafts of morning light finding their way between the tiniest gap in the curtains, felt like icicles piercing her eyes.

She and Iris had discovered the sideboard in the dining room had a section filled with bottles of brandy, whisky, gin and vodka, so either the man did have friends somewhere in Clementine Cove or close by, or he liked his drink.

Iris had opened a bottle of brandy and poured them both large glasses. And then another glass each. And then one more, just because they liked it. So by the time Elodie finally went back to her room, she was sure she could see two beds, but she wasn't sure which one of them she should get into. A tentative hand held out in front of her found that there was only one and she clambered into it and went straight to sleep.

She awoke with a headache from hell, the icicles of light piercing her eyes ... and Iris thumping on her bedroom door.

'You awake, El?'

'I'm awake,' she groaned, one hand against her head as if the thing might fall off if she didn't hang onto it. 'There's no need to shout.'

Iris shoved the door open, grinning broadly. 'What's up? Have you got a headache?'

'Haven't you?'

Elodie glared at her. At least Iris was bringing coffee. Elodie could smell the wonderful aroma as she tried to sit up in bed.

'Nope. I'm feeling fine. Apart from the bloody weather. You won't believe this but it's absolutely chucking it down again. In fact, if anything, it's raining even harder than yesterday.'

Iris put the mug of steaming coffee on Elodie's bedside table, together with two headache tablets, and leapt onto the bed, sprawling out at Elodie's feet.

Elodie grimaced as Iris' weight on the mattress made it rock. It might've been the slightest of movements at any other time but right now it made Elodie feel as if she were on the deck of a ship in a very stormy sea.

'Thanks for these.' Elodie swallowed the tablets one after the other and washed them down with a swig of coffee. It was only then that she noticed Iris was fully dressed. 'How long have you been up?'

Iris shrugged. 'About an hour or so. I slept like a log but woke up really early and then I couldn't get back to sleep. I was tempted to go and start reading those files. But I knew you would never forgive me if I did that without telling you.'

'Too right! I'm still not sure we should read them. Part of me thinks we should just have a massive bonfire and burn the lot.'

Iris pushed herself up onto one elbow, an astonished look in her eyes.

'Are you serious?'

Elodie nodded. 'Yes. From what we know of your uncle, those files don't contain anything good. Surely if we read them, it makes us no better than him? Do you really want to know all the deep, dark secrets of everyone in Clementine Cove?'

Iris furrowed her brows and thought about it while Elodie sipped her coffee.

'Are you honestly telling me, El that you're not even slightly curious what Archer's file says about him?'

Elodie sighed. 'Of course I'm curious. I told you I was last night. But as I also said last night, I still think it's wrong for us to read them.'

'Hmm. I do agree with you, but part of me really wants to find out exactly what Stanley knew about everyone and, more importantly, whether he had used any of that knowledge to his advantage. You know what Mum and Dad said last night about Stanley trying to blackmail Mum. We briefly discussed it last night but what if it is true? What if he was blackmailing some, if not all, of the residents of this village? If we knew that, we could tell them all that they don't have to worry about it anymore because we certainly won't be blackmailing them.'

Elodie pulled a face. 'Neither will Stanley now he's dead. I can see the sense in what you're saying, but, more importantly, we could always tell everyone that we found some files and we've destroyed them. And I think we should also say that we didn't read them. Because I still don't think we should, Iris.'

Iris huffed. 'Sometimes you can be far too sensible to be fun. Okay. I'll try to stop myself from reading them. As for destroying them, I don't think we should do that. Strictly speaking, everything in this cottage now belongs to my dad, including those files. If we destroyed them, we would be destroying his property. We have to tell him and Mum about them. And I think we have to do whatever Dad says.'

'I suppose that's true. I hadn't thought about it like that. But after what happened to your mum and dad, I have a feeling they will probably want to get rid of them.'

'Sadly, I think you're right. They'll probably tell us to do what you suggested. Burn them. We'll call them this evening and tell them what we found. It's about 5 a.m. in the Caribbean, so they probably won't thank us if we call them now, and I know they said they were going on a day trip today. I don't want to spoil that. And besides, they won't be able to talk surrounded by a group of other holidaymakers. We'll wait until later when they can have the privacy of their suite.'

'That makes sense. And I suppose there's no real rush.'

Iris rolled herself off the bed and stood up, making Elodie feel seasick once again.

'I suppose I'll just have to find some other way to entertain myself. Now are you ever going to get up? It's almost 9 and, as it's pouring hard, we could spend the morning putting those decorations up because we didn't do them last night.'

'Is it really worth it? We're leaving tomorrow.'

Iris looked horrified. 'Elodie Abbott! What on earth is wrong with you? You must be ill. Since when have you not wanted to put up decorations?'

'I'm hung over.'

'That's never stopped you before.'

Elodie shrugged and finished her coffee, placing the mug on the bedside table. She pulled her knees towards her chest, hugging them tight, and rested her chin on her clasped hands.

'I'm not really in a Christmassy mood at the moment. And yes. You're probably right. Maybe I am ill. I know this isn't at all like me. I don't know what's wrong, but I had the strangest dreams. Nightmares really. And I just don't feel ... as excited as I did yesterday.'

'This weather doesn't help,' Iris said, opening the curtains.

'Arghh! Close those curtains.'

There wasn't much daylight hidden amongst the heavy gunmetal grey clouds and sheets of torrential rain but what little there was made Elodie's eyes hurt.

Iris did as asked. 'I know what you need.' She spun round and beamed at Elodie. 'A full English breakfast, followed by another trip to Millside. I'm sure there were some stalls we didn't visit at the Christmas Market yesterday.'

That did sound appealing, even with a headache. Especially the full English breakfast. The fast-acting headache tablets seemed to be working their magic and a hot, invigorating shower would help.

'Okay,' Elodie said, easing back the duvet as if it weighed several kilos and gingerly swinging her legs over the side of the bed. 'Give me twenty minutes.'

Iris laughed. 'I knew food and shopping would work, although I'm still surprised putting up decorations didn't. I'll be downstairs.'

Chapter 12

After showering, Elodie dressed in black trousers and another Christmas-themed sweater and hurried downstairs to meet Iris. It had only taken her fifteen minutes, the thought of a full English breakfast making her hurry.

'Did you notice yesterday which of the cafés in the shopping centre does breakfasts?' she asked, taking her mug into the kitchen and placing it in the dishwasher, which was where they had put their glasses and plates from yesterday.

Iris had an odd expression on her face. 'What if we have breakfast at the Cove Café?'

Elodie frowned. 'O-k-ay. But why? Marian might not be that pleased to see us again, and if we're going shopping at Millside, wouldn't it make more sense for us to have breakfast there?'

'It would. But I've been thinking.'

Elodie tutted and then laughed. 'Oh dear. Why do I get the feeling I'm not going to like this?'

'Because you're probably not. But it makes perfect sense to me. What if we casually mention that we found some files in Stanley's study, and that they had names written on the tabs, and see how she reacts? That way we'll know whether or not she knew about them. If Stanley was blackmailing her, or anything like that, she'll realise he probably kept that information in those files, and she'll also realise there's a file on her.'

'That's true. But won't she then think that we've read them? She might not be happy about that.'

'Okay. We could add that we haven't read them. We just saw the names.'

'I'd prefer that.'

'Something else occurred to me though.' Iris now looked a little sheepish.

'Y-e-s?'

'While you were in the shower I got a text from Jill. She's the travel agent who organised Mum and Dad's trip and who I asked to book that helicopter flight for them as a surprise present from me, remember? She was texting to confirm it's tomorrow.'

Elodie nodded. 'Yes. They'll be thrilled. Er ... But what's that got to do with this?'

Iris sucked in a breath and let it out. 'We both assumed, because of what we know about Stanley, and because of the odd reactions we got yesterday, that all those files relate to some sort of nefarious activity on his part. But what if they don't? I mean, I don't suppose for one minute that this is the case, but what if Stanley was a travel agent who worked from home? Like Jill. Or ... a financial adviser, or an accountant, or something like that? And what if all those files simply contain information related to Stanley's job? I know you don't want to look at them but, perhaps before we do anything else, we should. Or at least look at one. Just to make sure they're what we both believe they are and not something completely innocent and above board.'

Elodie couldn't negate that reasoning but she wasn't sure whether she felt relieved or slightly disappointed.

'That's possible. Of course it is. I don't know why we didn't think of that straight away.'

Iris frowned. 'Except ... Why would there be different coloured files? And why aren't they simply alphabetical?'

'Because ... Ooh! Because some of them are VIP clients and some are new ones and the rest are sort of in between. So the files range in colour based on the amount of business they gave him, or the value of that business or ... something.'

Iris nodded her head from side to side.

'That's possible. However, I still think it's unlikely. But what I'm going to suggest is this. I think we should look at one file.' She held up her hand to indicate that Elodie should wait until she had finished. 'Just one. A grey one. Because we both agree we think the grey ones are the least important. And we pick a name that we don't know. Which isn't difficult because we've only met a few of the villagers so far. We read just as much as we need to in order to discover whether the file is to do with an innocent business transaction ... or something else. Or ... We do as I said earlier, and go to Cove Café, tell Marian about the files and see how she reacts.'

'Both options are giving me an unpleasant taste in my mouth.'

Iris smirked. 'That's not the options. That's too much alcohol last night.'

Elodie grinned in spite of the seriousness of the situation. 'You may be right. I really need to eat.' She made a decision. 'I think we go with option two. Or do I mean option one? The one where we go to the café and see how Marian reacts. That way we don't have to read any of the files. If they are to do with Stanley's job and are all related to innocent business transactions, Marian will tell us. She'll say something like, 'Oh yes. Stanley handled all my holidays.' Or, 'Stanley did my accounts.' Or whatever.'

Iris laughed. 'And if she doesn't say that, but just keeps quiet. Or worse still, throws us out, we'll know those files are probably far from innocent dealings. Okay. I'll go along with that. But I get the feeling that at some stage, whether you want to do so or not, we're going to have to bite the bullet and look inside one of those files.'

Chapter 13

Once again Elodie and Iris drove to Cove Close and parked right outside Cove Café which was as empty this morning as it had been yesterday.

Marian was wiping a table and turned towards the door as the doormat played Jingle Bells, her smile faltering when she saw who had triggered the cheery tune, but it was back in place within a matter of seconds. She was probably glad to have customers, no matter who they were.

'Good morning,' she said, doing a very good job of pretending they were welcome. 'Sit wherever you like. I'm not expecting to be busy today. It may be a Saturday but this weather is appalling. And, of course, there's the Christmas Market at Millside. This close to Christmas a lot of my customers go there. Not much point in them traipsing down here if that's where they're going for their Christmas shopping. I love this village but the lack of shops on this side of Moneymaker Circle means that small businesses like mine don't get quite as much custom at this time of year as we do in the summer months, especially when the weather is like this.'

She seemed to be rambling. Was that because she felt awkward after yesterday? Or was it because she was upset by her lack of customers and felt a need to vent her frustration regardless of who the recipient might be?

'We're going to Millside later,' Iris said, somewhat tactlessly, 'but first we need breakfast and we thought we'd come here.'

'It avoids the queues, I suppose.' Marian looked downhearted.

'That wasn't the reason.'

'No,' Elodie said, stepping in before Iris had a chance to say something both of them might regret. 'We came here because the food we had yesterday was delicious.'

Now the smile on Marian's face was genuine, even though they had only had the clementine and cranberry Christmas muffins yesterday, and those were probably made elsewhere.

'It's a shame you're only here for the weekend,' Marian said.

'We were thinking the same,' said Elodie. 'And this morning I would like ...' She glanced at the specials on the blackboard.

'Marian's mega breakfast, please. What is that, exactly? I suppose I should've asked before I ordered it.'

Marian laughed. 'It's a full English breakfast but it comes with two sausages, two rashers of bacon and two eggs instead of one of each in the standard breakfast. You also get two slices of toast, white or wholemeal, butter and your choice of marmalade or jams. It also comes with a large mug of tea or coffee, but if you prefer hot chocolate you can have that instead. Although I will have to charge a little bit more if you want the melting snowman hot chocolate you had yesterday.'

'No thanks,' Elodie said. 'Today I need coffee. Lots and lots of coffee. Iris and I foolishly opened a bottle of brandy last night.'

'Then you definitely need my mega breakfast.' Marian winked at her. 'And what about you, Iris? Do you need my mega breakfast and lots of coffee?'

Iris grinned. 'Luckily for me, I'm not hung over. But yes. I'll have the same as El, please.'

'Take a seat then, ladies, and I'll bring it over shortly.'

Elodie followed Iris to the window seat they had occupied the day before and they removed their damp coats. Despite having parked right outside the café, and running the few feet from the car, they had still got wet.

Marian disappeared into the kitchen and Elodie and Iris stared out across the bay, which today, in spite of the once again torrential rain was more visible than it had been yesterday.

Brightly coloured sailboats bobbed in the marina and one or two gulls flew overhead, but other than that, the bay was deserted. The sea, which no doubt looked glorious in the summer, was a rippling, slate grey.

From their table, Elodie could see Clementine Cottage and its gardens to the left of the café. Hope Head, with the church of St Mary's in the Wood perched near the edge of the steep and rocky cliff, were opposite, with Rosehip Cottage nestled behind the church and only just visible. Beside the church and rectory were a few lanes and several pretty, pastel-coloured cottages.

The lighthouse just behind Arrow Point, the equally rocky but less steep promontory opposite Hope Head, was clearly visible today, it's light shining out through the rain.

And the pub. Archer Rhodes' pub, The Bow and Quiver, with its bright blue façade and thatched roof, sat proudly beside a small copse and a surprisingly large Christmas tree, adorned with what, from where she sat, looked to Elodie, very much like bottles. Presumably empty.

'Are those bottles hanging on that Christmas tree beside the pub?' she asked.

Iris, who had her back to that part of the view, turned on her seat and squinted into the distance.

'They look bottle shaped to me. But they could be proper Christmas decorations. I've seen loads of bottle shaped ornaments this year. And glasses too. Wine glasses, champagne flutes, cocktail glasses. You name it, you can get an ornament in it.'

'They're real bottles,' Marian said, appearing from the kitchen with two massive, Christmas-themed mugs of coffee, along with a huge smile. 'It was Archer's idea. When he was a kid, about ten, I think, he found a bottle washed up on the beach in the bay, with a message in it. It had come all the way from Perth in Australia, and the sender had written a note and placed it in a sealed plastic bag, asking whoever found it to contact them at the address on the note. Naturally, Archer did and ... Er ... But that's another story.' She looked slightly anxious for a moment and shook her head as if ridding herself of an unpleasant memory. 'A few years later around this time of year and when he was sixteen, he ... er ... got very drunk, and he wrote a note. Well, I believe it was more of a wish than a note. Anyway, he stuck it in his empty vodka bottle, tied a red ribbon around the neck, and hung it on the Christmas tree. When he saw it there the next day, he went to take it down, but after his parents hauled him over the coals for downing a bottle of vodka, albeit only a 35 CL bottle which only had about six measures of vodka left in it when he drank it, they asked him what was inside it. He told them, that in his drunken state of mind, he'd made a wish, stuck it in the bottle and tied it to the tree, hoping for some sort of Christmas miracle or something. They thought it was a lovely gesture, so they persuaded him to leave it up and not only that, they told everyone about it ... much to Archer's disgust at the time. But everyone loved the idea so much that it became a tradition. And now, every year, we all write out a wish, put it in an empty bottle. One that we've bought at Archer's pub, of course, and we hang them on the tree. But it might be better if you didn't tell him I've told you the whole story. He's a bit ... sensitive about it. Just tell him I said that making a wish, putting it in a bottle and tying it to the tree is a village tradition.'

Elodie didn't think Marian *had* told them the whole story. There was definitely something she had left out. Something relating to the writer of the original note that he'd found on the beach, perhaps? Or something that happened when Archer was between the ages of ten and sixteen, maybe? Elodie couldn't help but wonder what the rest of the story was.

'We should do that,' Iris said, excitement written all over her face, her gingerbread men earrings dancing enthusiastically as if they were as excited as Iris.

'Yes,' Elodie agreed. 'Although I think my bottle might have to be something non-alcoholic.'

Iris laughed and so did Marian.

'Hair of the dog,' Marian joked.

'You'll be fine by this evening,' Iris said. 'Does the pub serve food, Marian?'

'It does. Bentley is the chef and he's a bloody good one. Nothing fancy. Well, not too fancy. He does a Stroganoff to kill for, and his Coq au Vin – Oooooh. On my life, you'll think you've died and gone to heaven.'

'Fantastic! Let's go there for dinner tonight, El? Oh. Do we need to book?'

Marian nodded. 'It's popular. Especially on a Saturday night so you might not get in. Give him a call and see.' She wrote down a number on her notepad, tore off the page and handed it to Iris with a broad grin. 'You never know. If you tell him you're the girls he saw in here yesterday, he might find a table for you.' The grin slid from her face. 'Er. But as I said. It's popular, so maybe you should try somewhere else instead. I'll get your breakfasts. You'll want to be off soon to do your Christmas shopping.'

It was as if she had suddenly remembered that Elodie and Iris were as good as lepers, as she hurried away to the kitchen.

'That was weird,' Iris said, leaning across the table and lowering her voice.

'It was. But she was like that yesterday. One minute, all chatty and friendly, the next like a block of ice and then she melted slightly and was friendly again. Today, she was ice, then friendly and now the freeze has set in.'

'And what about the story she told us about Archer?' Iris lowered her voice even more. 'She didn't tell us everything, did she? I got the feeling there's more to that than she said.'

'Me too. But, if those files in the study are what we think they are, we now know how Stanley might've found out about people's secret wishes, don't we? Other than by simply watching them, I mean.'

'I suppose that's true.' Iris looked thoughtful. 'Although surely someone would've seen him if he read all the notes.

And that looks like a massive tree so he'd probably need a ladder to reach some of them. Someone definitely would've seen that. He couldn't just turn up outside the pub with a ladder under his arm and plonk it against the Christmas tree without being spotted.'

Elodie grinned at the image forming in her head. 'How did the people who wrote those ones near the top get them up there?'

Iris shrugged. 'Archer, I suppose. He might offer to hang them. Perhaps he has to do that. You know, because of all the stupid Health and Safety regulations. If someone fell while hanging a bottle on his Christmas tree, they might sue him, or something. He might be breaking all sorts of rules by even doing this.'

'Maybe that's what's in his file, d'you think?'

Iris pulled a face. 'No, El. I think, if those files are what we suspect, and bearing in mind Archer's file is red ... and thick ... I think Stanley has a whole lot more on the guy than just breaking a few rules and regulations. Although, I suppose, even a minor infraction could cause Archer to lose his liquor licence, so maybe. Oh, I don't know. It's all just speculation. I know how you feel about it but we really need to read those files.'

'But …' Elodie let her voice trail off as Marian appeared from the kitchen.

'Here you are,' Marian said, carrying two large plates to the table. 'Enjoy. I'll be in the kitchen if you need anything.'

'Actually, Marian,' Iris said, 'may I ask you a quick question?'

Marian looked as if she'd turned to stone.

'A question? What sort of question? I mean. Er. Yes. I suppose so.'

Iris squirted ketchup over her breakfast, looking calm and casual and as if she was about to ask the way to somewhere.

'I wondered if you knew what my uncle did for a living.' She ignored Marian's gasp. 'We assume he worked from home because we found some files in his study, but we haven't looked at them yet.'

Marian seemed to be having difficulty breathing.

'Files? In his study?'

'Yes. We took a quick peek inside one of the drawers of his filing cabinets and the files in there had tabs with names written on them, so we assume he must have had clients or something. But I'd never met my uncle and I know nothing about him other than my family fell out with him years ago and haven't spoken to him for at least thirty-six years. My mum says my dad is nothing at all like his brother. That they're as different as chalk and cheese.'

'They did? They haven't? They are? Um. Oh. I see. Well, that's a different matter then, I suppose. Or it may be. Er. No. Sorry. No idea. I didn't really know him that well.'

'I see. Okay. Thanks anyway.'

'Are you ... are you going to look at them? The files, I mean?'

Iris shrugged. 'I doubt it. I was just curious. But what he did for a job isn't really important. At least not to me. And we're only here for the weekend. We just came to get the keys and to make sure the place is secure, that the heating's kept on so the pipes don't burst, and to sort a few things out. My parents are on holiday at the moment and they won't be back until after Christmas. They'll probably come down in the New Year and decide what to do with the cottage and its contents, including the files, then. Thanks though. This looks delicious.'

Marian hovered beside the table for a moment or two as if she wanted to say more but when Elodie smiled at her, she fiddled with her apron and dashed off towards the kitchen.

'So,' Iris said, 'Marian may or may not have known about the files. I'm leaning towards, not. But she was definitely a little worried, don't you think?'

'A little worried?' Elodie frowned at Iris. 'At one point there I thought the poor woman might have a heart attack. Yes. I'd say she's worried. And more than a little. She might not have known Stanley kept files, but I'm fairly sure she knew what he was up to.'

Chapter 14

'I can't believe you almost missed the turn off to the shopping centre yet again!' Elodie exclaimed, with one hand clinging to her seatbelt and the other pressed against the dashboard as Iris did a manoeuvre that was something between an emergency stop and one of those hand brake turns that always look impressive in films but in reality, aren't. Not if you're a passenger. 'It's a good thing there's nothing behind us.'

'Sorry,' Iris said. 'My mind was elsewhere.'

'That's comforting.' Elodie rolled her eyes.

Iris laughed. 'The place looks busy. Keep your eyes open for a parking space.'

'It's Saturday morning, and after today there's only one more Saturday till Christmas. Did you expect it to be empty?'

Iris threw her a sideways glance. 'What's up with you? You're getting stroppy.'

'No, I'm not.' Elodie let out a sigh. 'Okay. Perhaps I am, a little. I can't stop thinking about that thick red file on Archer Rhodes. If we're assuming red is bad and thick is really bad, it just doesn't make sense. He seemed like a nice guy. And yes, I'm fully aware we don't really know anything about him, but the way he acted yesterday and the things he said, plus what Marian just told us about him finding that bottle on the beach and writing to the sender, and the stuff about hanging those bottles with messages in on the Christmas tree outside the pub, don't add up. That was all so sweet.'

'Almost too sweet,' Iris giggled.

'It was romantic.'

'He was ten when he answered the note. I don't think romance came into it. And you don't know what he wished for when he was sixteen. He might have wished he could get lucky with some girl. That's neither sweet nor romantic.'

Elodie tutted. 'Trust you to think the worst. Besides Marian said he told his parents what he'd wished for and they were pleased. So pleased in fact that the whole bottle thing became a tradition. So maybe he wished for world peace.'

'Ah yes. That old chestnut.'

'Iris! World peace is not an old chestnut. It's something we should all aspire to.'

'Yeah, yeah. Are you actually looking for parking spaces?'

'Yes.' Elodie wasn't, but neither was she going to admit that to Iris. Fortunately, she spotted one directly ahead. 'Look! There's one.'

Iris sped up and, ignoring the car to the right of the space that had its reversing lights on, she drove in and parked.

An irate woman got out of the other car and yelled, 'We were just about to park there!'

'Were you?' Iris said, getting out of the car and smiling at the woman. 'Sorry about that, but we got here first.'

'We were reversing!'

'Now you don't have to.'

'You're not going to move?'

'Er. No. I'm sure there are plenty of other spaces.'

The woman glowered at Iris. Elodie was about to suggest that maybe they should let the woman have the space, but with a few expletives hanging in the air, the woman got back in her car and sped off.

'Merry Christmas!' Iris called after her.

'Perhaps we should have moved,' Elodie said.

Iris shook her head and laughed. 'You snooze, you lose. As you said yourself, El, counting today, there are only two more

Saturdays until Christmas. And I am not spending this one driving round this damn car park.'

'Coo-ey!' A voice called out.

Elodie and Iris spun round and Elodie groaned as Reverend Wilfred Parker and his sister Rosie came hurrying towards them.

'Are you all right?' Wilfred asked. 'We couldn't help but overhear the foul language that woman used. Sadly, some people need lessons in civility.'

'Er. We're fine, thanks,' Iris said. 'And it wasn't really her fault. I might have pinched her parking space. Although I didn't realise she was going to park here. I didn't actually see her until she got out of the car.'

At least Iris had the decency to look and sound humble, but Elodie wondered if she should question Iris' eyesight. Although, to be fair, Elodie hadn't seen the other car either until Iris was about to drive into the space.

'Oh, I see. That still doesn't excuse bad language.' A smile replaced his frown. 'Are you here to do some Christmas shopping? Rosie and I are.'

Elodie half expected Iris to say something sarcastic, but instead she merely smiled and said, 'That's nice.'

'Nice is hardly the word I would use,' Rosie said, sounding none too happy.

'Christmas shopping on the second to last Saturday before the big event is not exactly my idea of fun. But Will wanted to come and take a look at the Christmas Market so here we are. Not that it's going to be any different from last year's. Same old tat and overpriced rubbish, barely edible food, and sickly-sweet concoctions that would no doubt remove all trace of limescale from one's loo.'

'Rosie!' Wilfred's laugh sounded anything but jolly. 'Sometimes you do say the most dreadful things.'

Rosie rolled her eyes.

'We were sorry to see you left the tree lighting so early yesterday,' he continued. 'I was hoping to have a word.'

'Just one?' Iris asked, straight-faced.

Elodie stifled a giggle and Wilfred looked confused.

'Your sense of humour is similar to Stanley's,' Rosie said. 'You may not have met your uncle, but you clearly have several things in common. Like your ability to sing, for example.'

Elodie and Iris exchanged surprised glances. Had Rosie searched for Iris' name on the internet? How else could she know about Iris' talent?

'Oh yes,' Wilfred said, a wan smile on his face. 'It seems you were telling porky pies. Just like Stanley, you clearly have the voice of an angel.' He tutted twice and wagged a finger at Iris.

'Did you look me up?'

'I did,' Rosie said, without a hint of embarrassment.

'Actually,' Iris said, a strange grin forming on her mouth. 'It's good that we bumped into you. You were friends with my uncle, weren't you? Do you know what he did for a living?'

'A living?' Wilfred glanced at his sister. 'I don't believe he did anything, did he?'

'Really? Only we found several files in his study and they appear to have names on each of them. We haven't looked inside them ...' Iris shot a look at Elodie and grinned. 'Yet. But we assumed he might be an accountant, or a financial adviser, or an insurance salesman.' She laughed. 'Or maybe he sold double glazing. He certainly had a thing for windows and window seats.'

Wilfred shook his head, looking even more confused. 'Names? Of people?'

'Yes. I even think I spotted one with Parker written on it. But I might have been mistaken.'

Rosie's gasp was audible but she turned it into a cough and patted her chest as the colour rose above the make-up on her face.

'Goodness me. I seem to have a tickle in my throat. I think I need to find some water. Please excuse us.'

'Of course,' Elodie said. 'I hope you're okay.'

'I have water in the car, dear,' Wilfred said, taking Rosie by the elbow and, with a quick wave and a, 'Bye for now,' he led her away.

Iris beamed at Elodie. 'I think we can safely say that Rosie is as worried as Marian.'

Elodie nodded. 'But the vicar wasn't, was he? He just seemed confused. Which is odd, isn't it? If I remember correctly, Marian's file was blue, Wilfred's was pink, and Rosie's was orange and thicker than her brother's. Working on the basis that pink is slightly worse than blue, if Marian is worried, then the vicar should be too.'

Iris nodded. 'I agree. Maybe blue is worse than pink? Oh I don't know. Let's just go and do some Christmas shopping. I think I need some more Christmassy earrings.'

Elodie laughed. 'Firstly, I think you bought the entire stock yesterday. And secondly, there aren't enough days between now and Christmas for you to wear all the earrings you've already got.'

'I've decided it should be Christmas every day. And I've also decided we need to find some Christmassy earrings for you.'

'Easier said than done, with clip-ons. And no. Not my ears. Clip-on earrings, as you well know.'

Iris laughed. 'You spoil all my jokes. I still don't know why you won't get your ears pierced.'

'Because needles terrify me. And besides, if we were meant to have holes in our earlobes we would've been born with them.' Elodie grinned.

Iris tutted. 'I don't know about falling for Archer Rhodes. You should marry the vicar. All you've done so far this weekend is give me sermons and preach to me about what's right and wrong.'

But she was laughing as she linked her arm through Elodie's.

Chapter 15

Elodie planned to take her time getting ready for the evening. She'd even bought another new dress while they were at the shopping centre. She wanted to look her best if they were going to Archer's pub for dinner – which still wasn't definite. When they phoned the pub to book, using the number Marian had given them, they got through to an answering machine, on which they'd left a message together with Elodie's phone number, but so far, Archer hadn't called back.

And she didn't know why looking good tonight was so important. She and Iris were only here for the weekend. No matter how much Elodie might like the idea, it was very unlikely that she could hook up with Archer tonight. She didn't even know if he might want to hook up with her. He might not be remotely interested.

But if the looks he'd given her, both in the café yesterday and later at the rectory – before the announcement Rosie made about Iris' relationship to Stanley – were anything to go by, it was possible that he was as keen on the idea as she was.

Except the look he'd given her as he'd left the cocktail party had been far from lustful. It had been as cold as the ice at the North Pole.

Why did that depress her?

It wasn't as if she was that desperate to have sex.

But as an image of Archer's face popped into her head, she realised that wasn't true.

Right now, as she stood naked in the shower, she could think of nothing she would rather be doing than having sex with Archer Rhodes. Even if the man was basically a stranger.

And a stranger with a thick, red file, lurking in one of Stanley Talbot's cabinets.

She washed the conditioner from her hair and stepped out onto the mat, grabbing a thick, fluffy towel from the heated towel rail and wrapping it around her.

She had to get Archer out of her head. The last time she'd felt like this about a man, it had eventually ended in disaster.

She dried her hair and pondered the past.

How could Ben have lied to her the way he had? How could he have deceived her every single day for two whole years and not been in the least bit bothered by his lies?

But more importantly, how could she not have seen it? Not suspected a thing?

When he'd told her he had to work away for part of the week, and also, often at weekends, she hadn't doubted for one minute that that was what he was doing. Working.

And clearly, the other woman in his life had believed him too. He must've told her the same.

And then he had proposed and Elodie had been over the moon.

Her sister wasn't though. And come to think of it, neither were her parents. Or Iris. They all questioned whether he was really The One. They'd asked her if she was absolutely sure she wanted to marry him. She brushed away their doubts. Doubts that weren't based on anything other than 'a feeling he might not be right for you' as her sister had said.

Why hadn't she listened to them? Especially to her sister. Like Elodie herself, Sasha often got 'a feeling' about something. And those 'feelings', more often than not, were spot on.

Sasha had experienced one of her 'feelings' the moment she met her husband. She told Elodie that she knew he was The One for her the second he stepped onto that train and looked her directly in the eye.

But that was three years after they discovered Ben was a liar and a cheat.

Like Elodie herself, not one of them had suspected for a moment that he had another fiancée; they just thought he was wrong for her, somehow. Unfortunately, Elodie hadn't agreed. Until someone popped an envelope through her door. An envelope containing photos of Ben with another woman.

When she'd questioned him, it all eventually came tumbling out. Although he did try to lie his way out of it for a day or two.

'I love you, Ellie,' he'd said, using his pet name for her. No one other than Ben had ever called her Ellie. Iris called her El and so did her sister and sometimes her parents, but nobody called her Ellie ... except Ben. 'This woman's just a friend from work. And we're not kissing, exactly. It was just one of those pecks on the cheek, except we both misjudged it and ended up kissing one another on the lips. How whoever took that photo managed to catch us at that precise second is beyond me.'

Elodie had believed him at first, because she had wanted to so much. But her own feelings were telling her that something wasn't right. She had asked Ben to introduce her to the woman, maybe even ask this colleague to join them for a drink. That was when Ben finally realised the game was up and Elodie discovered the astonishing truth.

Even then he tried to convince her to stay with him, telling her once more how much he loved her.

'But the problem is, Ellie, I love her too. I thought I'd be able to choose between you, but so far I can't. Just give me time and I will. I promise. And I think it's going to be you.'

Elodie still couldn't believe that was what he'd said. As if she should think herself lucky that he might pick her. That all she had to do was wait patiently for him to decide. It was a wonder she hadn't hit him with a heavy object. That was what Iris wanted to do. She'd threatened to if he ever darkened El's door again.

Elodie hadn't said anything at first. She hadn't been able to speak. She couldn't take in it. How could this have happened? How could this be true? They were engaged, for pity's sake. But he was also engaged to *her*.

Eventually, Elodie knew what to say and what to do.

'Get lost, Ben,' she'd said. 'I never want to see or hear from you again.'

But it had broken her heart into a million tiny pieces and she wasn't sure she'd be able to find them all and stick it back together again. It had turned her world upside down and since that day she had never again fallen in love with anyone. Never felt the way she had about Ben. Yet she still compared boyfriends to him. Or she had done so until now.

Until the moment Archer Rhodes had walked into Cove Café and looked her directly in the eye.

She hadn't compared Archer to anyone when she'd seen him yesterday. Why was that? Was it because he was ... incomparable? At least to any man she had ever met before.

And now she was considering – no, not considering – hoping that a complete stranger with dark hair of the richest brown she had ever seen and a smile warm enough to melt the biggest iceberg might be as attracted to her as she was to him.

A man whose name was written on a thick red file, which could only mean one thing. Archer Rhodes had a secret. Or maybe more than one. And falling for him was a dangerous thing to do.

The problem was, she was pretty sure there wasn't very much she could do to stop herself from falling for him. It was just a good thing she and Iris were only here for the weekend.

She applied her make-up carefully. Her new dress was a rich, deep scarlet mini; her lips and nails had to match. She studied her reflection in the mirror and a warm glow seemed to surround her. Or maybe that was merely the light from the angle of the lamp beside her.

'El?' Iris yelled up the stairs. 'Are you going to be ready anytime this century? Christmas will have been and gone by the time we go out to dinner.'

Chapter 16

Archer looked surprised to see them when Elodie and Iris walked into The Bow and Quiver. He was pulling a pint and chatting to a customer but he glanced up as they opened the door and for a moment, he seemed to freeze. And it wasn't just because of the blast of icy air that swept in with them as they stepped inside.

The expression on Archer's face was one of delight at first but it quickly changed to concern as his dark brows knit together and the warm and gorgeous smile slid into a grimace. His hand seemed to tighten on the beer pump as he looked from Elodie back to his customer, his face now set in a firm, cold and unwelcoming scowl.

'Hey Archer!' the customer said. 'Wanna stop now?'

Archer stared at the beer pouring over his hand from the glass he'd overfilled.

'Shit!' he said, so loud that several of the other customers in the pub turned and looked at him. 'Sorry, Dave. I'll pour you another.' He put the glass to one side, took a clean glass from the shelf behind him and with a quick glance towards the half open door where Elodie and Iris still stood, uncertain whereabouts the restaurant area was, he said, 'Are you coming in, or not? I don't care which, but close that bloody door.'

And all eyes turned to Elodie and Iris.

'Hello to you too,' Elodie said, a little louder than she had intended.

But honestly. Did the man have to be so rude? It wasn't quite the reception she had hoped for.

Archer shot her a look, raised one eyebrow and a slight smile tugged at the corner of his mouth but he quickly checked it.

'We booked a table for dinner,' Iris said, walking towards the bar but stopping when she realised Elodie wasn't following her. She reached back and tugged at Elodie's sleeve.

'Did you?'

Archer didn't bother to look up. He handed Dave the replacement beer he had poured, took the money given to him and rang it through the till.

Elodie cleared her throat.

'We phoned this morning and left a message.'

'Did anyone call you back?'

This time he didn't even bother to turn around.

'No. But ... Oh. Was someone supposed to?'

She was well aware that someone was, but she and Iris had hoped it wouldn't matter.

Now Archer turned and leant both elbows on the bar.

'That's why the message said, "someone will get back to you, but if they don't, you will need to call again, or try to book your table via the website." I checked the website for bookings at 5 this evening and I don't recall seeing your names.'

She had missed the bit about the website. She had been so flustered by hearing his soft and sexy voice on the answering machine and so intent on trying to sound equally sexy and sultry herself, that she hadn't taken that bit in.

'Are ... are you saying you don't have a table for us?'

'Not if you haven't booked. Believe it or not, this place is popular.' He gave a little shrug and a half-hearted smile.

Elodie's mouth fell open but she couldn't think of anything to say. Fortunately, Iris could.

'What about if we wait for a table? And while we wait we can have that free drink you offered us yesterday.'

They had reached the bar and Iris stepped into the space Dave had vacated, grinning broadly at Archer as she did so.

He hesitated for just a second and then turned, took two menus from another shelf behind him and handed them to Iris.

'Fine. But you may have a long wait.'

'That's okay,' Iris said. 'We have nowhere else we need to be. And this is such a warm and welcoming place.'

Archer clearly picked up on Iris's sarcasm because his eyes narrowed a fraction as if her words had stung him, but he gave as good as he got.

'It is warm and welcoming, which is why it's so hard to get a table on a Saturday night. Unless you book in advance.'

'We tried that.' Iris smiled at him, but it wasn't her usual smile. 'It didn't work. Marian didn't tell us about the website and we must've missed that bit on your message.'

'Marian?' He seemed surprised as he shot a look at Elodie.

'Yes,' Elodie said. 'Marian told us the food here is fantastic. She gave us the number to call.'

He seemed to mellow slightly. 'I see.' He ran a hand through his lustrous brown hair. 'I might be able to find you a table in, say, half an hour. Does that work for you?'

Elodie beamed at him. 'That's perfect. Thank you.'

'Don't thank me yet. I only said "might". But in the meantime let me get you those drinks. What would you like?'

'I'll have a barrel of red wine,' Iris said, laughing. 'Oh sorry. Did you mean a glass?'

Archer's gorgeous smile appeared. 'I'd like to see you drink a barrel of red wine.'

'Be careful what you wish for,' said Iris.

The freeze began again. 'I'm always careful what I wish for. These days.'

That sounded as though it had some significance but Elodie chose not to ask.

'Iris and I drank virtually a barrel of brandy last night. At least it felt like that this morning.'

'Hangover?' Archer queried, a hint of sympathy in his eyes.

'The size of Jupiter.'

Archer raised his brows. 'That bad, huh? I've got a remedy for hangovers. I'll give it to you later. I can't stretch to a barrel of red, but will two large glasses suffice?'

Without waiting for a response he turned and opened a bottle of red wine, pouring two large glasses and sliding them across the bar to Elodie and Iris.

'We're happy to pay for them,' Elodie said, garnering an irritated look from Iris. 'We don't expect you to give free drinks to strangers.'

She had tried to make her voice sound friendly but also seductive, and she gave him what she hoped was her sexiest smile.

His smile beat hers by a mile, she was certain of that.

He looked her directly in the eye. 'Strangers are only friends you haven't met yet, or so my mum always said. And Yeats, I believe. But poetry isn't my thing.'

'So we're friends then? Because we've met. Three times now. But who's counting.'

She sounded like an idiot and Iris's loud tut and soft snort of laughter confirmed it.

'Here's to friendship then,' Iris said, as she raised her glass of wine and clinked it against Elodie's before raising it even higher in the air to Archer.

He picked up the discarded glass he had overfilled which contained a rich, copper coloured liquid, raised it in a toast, and nodded with a smile.

'To friendship,' he said, staring pointedly at Elodie.

'What's that you're drinking?' Iris queried.

'This is One for the Rhodes Ale. We brew it here. There's a micro-brewery in the back.' He nodded his head in that general direction.

'Wow!' Elodie said, impressed by his business acumen as much as by his looks and physique. 'A pub, a restaurant and a micro-brewery? Is there no end to your talents?' She meant it as a compliment but judging by the expression on his face he had taken it as sarcasm.

'We can't all be highly sought-after voice coaches or run hugely successful party stores online. Although as it happens, I do have other ... interests.'

Elodie and Iris exchanged glances.

'Did you look us up?' Iris queried.

Elodie was surprised. Clearly Stanley wasn't the only one who kept an eye on people in Clementine Cove.

Archer coloured up slightly. 'No. Nosy ... I mean, Rosie Parker mentioned it when she and Wilfred popped in at lunchtime.'

'Did she?' Iris said. 'That's interesting. Oh. Did she mention anything else? We bumped into them this morning at Millside.'

Archer looked thoughtful but slowly shook his head. 'I don't think so. Should she have?'

'Nope. I just thought she might. But I'll ask you myself.'

'Ask me what?'

Now he had a guarded expression and his eyes darted from Iris to Elodie and back to Iris.

'You were at the cocktail party and tree lighting, so you obviously heard that I am Stanley Talbot's niece. What you probably don't know is that I never met the man. There was a rift between him and my parents over thirty-six years ago. My dad is his brother. Was his brother, I should say. But they hadn't spoken since then and they were complete opposites in any event and never really got on.'

His dark brows furrowed and a lock of hair fell across his forehead as he tilted his head slightly to one side.

'Was that a question?'

'No.' Iris laughed. 'That was merely ... back story. This is the question. Did you know what Stanley did for a living?'

Archer tensed visibly. 'No idea. And I'd better get back to my customers.' He moved a few inches away from the bar but added, 'Why do you want to know?'

'Just curious really. We found several cabinets in Stanley's study and they were full of files. Different coloured files. All with people's names written on them. As I told

Nosy ... I mean, Rosie Parker, we haven't looked at them yet. And we're not really that interested. But I just thought I'd ask.'

His eyes narrowed, his jaw locked and his lips formed a tight line.

'Surely it would be easier to simply look at the files, wouldn't it? Or are they locked away? But then how would you know what they were?' He seemed to be mulling this over as he spoke. 'And what if ... the files aren't what you think they are? It might be wiser not to tell too many people what you've found.'

'That sounds rather ominous,' Elodie said.

'Almost like a threat,' Iris replied, a hint of laughter in her voice.

'Merely an observation.' Archer held Iris' gaze for a moment and then smiled at her and at Elodie. But the smile wasn't as warm as it had been. 'I must get on. Enjoy your drinks, ladies. I'll give you time to decide what you'd like to eat and I'll let you know when your table is ready.'

He walked away to serve the throng of customers waiting patiently for either Archer or one of his staff, to take their orders.

'He's a cool customer,' Iris said. 'I did notice him tense though. Did you?'

Elodie nodded, keeping her voice low. 'I still don't believe he's a bad guy. I don't care what anyone says. Look how popular this place is. How popular *he* is. Everyone seems to be smiling and laughing and happy. None of these people look as if they've got some deep dark secret, each worth being blackmailed for.'

She glanced around the pub and now she took in her surroundings. There appeared to be, not only the bar in which she and Iris and numerous others stood, but also two additional bars beyond, one of which might possibly be a restaurant section.

From the outside, with its bright blue façade, thatched roof, and Christmas tree strung with twinkling, multi-coloured lights and the red ribbons on those bottles containing messages, to the inside with the roaring log fire, pale blue walls, white ceilings and dark wooden beams from which warm, white lights glowed, the pub oozed charm.

The inglenook fireplace, as broad as it was high and the ancient oak mantle, resplendent in its festive greenery with an abundance of holly and mistletoe berries, made it even more welcoming than merely the logs crackling in the hearth.

The aged, misshapen wood tables and equally old, mismatched wooden chairs, together with the padded blue velvet seat cushions, various other patterned cushions and one or two throws strewn around, added to the warm and relaxing ambiance.

Added to all that, the cacophony of happy voices mingled with the Christmas songs ringing out from speakers placed high on the walls and hidden by more festive decorations, gave the impression that there was nothing but joy in the world, although this was anything but a silent night.

'I love this place,' Elodie said, meaning it.

'Yeah. It's certainly charming. Almost as charming as the owner. And unless I'm mistaken. Which I'm not. He's definitely interested in you.'

'What?'

Iris laughed. 'Oh come on, El. No secrets, remember? You can tell he is.'

Elodie grinned. 'I'm not sure. One minute I think he is, the next ... I don't know. Not that it matters. We're only here for one more night.'

'Isn't that a song? Who cares? I say, go for it. Don't worry about me.'

'I always worry about you,' Elodie joked. 'Especially today. I'm beginning to think you need your eyes tested.'

'Bloody hell!'

'I was joking, Iris!'

'What? Oh yeah. I didn't mean that. I meant *that*!'

She pointed to where a tall, broad shouldered, blond-haired man was leaning against a doorway behind the bar. He was wearing a T-shirt with an image of a reindeer carrying a frying pan printed on it, an apron with an image of several drunken reindeer in varying positions and a chef's hat with a smaller Santa hat pinned to the top. He was chatting with Archer who looked a lot happier than before.

'I assume that's Bentley,' Elodie said. 'The chef, Marian mentioned.'

'*That's* Bentley? Wow, El! You're not the only one who may well have fallen in love. We should've come here last night.'

Elodie couldn't have agreed more. But it was too late to think that now.

Chapter 17

Never one to miss an opportunity, or worry very much about what people might think of her, when Archer came to tell Elodie and Iris that their table was ready, fifteen minutes later, Iris didn't hesitate to ask Archer about the man they assumed was Bentley.

'If you'd like to follow me,' Archer said, 'I'll show you to your table.'

'El will follow you anywhere,' Iris said, causing Elodie to gasp with embarrassment.

Either Archer didn't hear, or he pretended not to because he said, 'Sorry Iris. What did you say?'

Elodie glowered a warning at her.

'I said we'll follow you anywhere.'

Archer gave Iris a curious look and an odd sort of smile.

'The restaurant is through here.'

He led them into what Elodie had assumed was another bar but it was in fact a cosy room with a smaller inglenook with a roaring fire at one end and a massive wooden barrel at the other.

On the flat top of the barrel was a silver pot in which stood cutlery wrapped in festive serviettes. A neat stack of equally festive napkins lay beside, together with small silver trays, each bearing a variety of condiments together with a sprig of freshly cut holly and a cute, ceramic robin.

There was also a beautiful crystal vase filled with a display of winter blooms and pine branches dotted with warm white fairy lights, in front of which was a cute, miniature Christmas village with lights in all the windows and a pair of ice skaters spinning around on a tiny pond.

Between the inglenook and the barrel there were several tables for two, some for four, and others sat six or eight.

Archer showed them to a solitary vacant table for two, close to the roaring log fire in the inglenook. It looked a little out of place, as if it had just been put there, possibly in a hurry, for Elodie and Iris.

'So,' Iris said, the moment she and Elodie sat down. 'Was that gorgeous blond hunk we saw you talking to just now, your chef, Bentley? And more importantly, is he single?'

Archer did a double take and made a sound something between a gasp and a snort of laughter.

'Excuse me?'

Iris gave a small sigh. 'I said–'

'I heard you.' Now Archer did laugh. 'I was just a bit surprised.'

Iris looked up at him. 'Why? Because you think I'm too forward?'

He laughed again. 'No. Because I don't think I've ever heard Bentley referred to as "a gorgeous blond hunk". A talented chef, yes. Even a good-looking guy. But a gorgeous blond hunk. That's a first. Anyway, to answer your question. Yes, it was. And yes, he is.'

'Thanks,' said Iris, grinning. 'Are you?'

Archer furrowed his brows. 'Am I ... what? Single?'

'Yep.'

Elodie felt the heat rise to her cheeks as he shot a look at her.

'Why do you ask? Isn't one guy enough for you?'

'Sorry,' Iris said, looking anything but apologetic. 'You're not my type. I go for big, blond and beautiful. Like Bentley. Not dark, moody and mysterious. That's El's type.'

This time as he looked Elodie, his gaze lingered.

'Really?' He dragged his gaze to Iris. 'Are you saying I'm dark, moody and mysterious?

Although I suppose a more pertinent question is, are you suggesting I'm the type of man Elodie might find interesting?'

'Absolutely not!' Elodie exclaimed. Although she had no idea why.

'She's lying,' Iris said. 'And yes, I was saying that. And yes you are.'

'Iris!' Elodie would have kicked Iris but she couldn't reach her under the table. 'She's joking, Archer. She's got a strange sense of humour.'

'That's a shame. I was hoping ...' His voice trailed off and as he gazed into Elodie's eyes, a slow and oh so sexy smile crept across his mouth. And then he seemed to remember where he was and gave a little cough. 'Have you decided what you'd like?'

Elodie couldn't speak. Her insides had turned to mush.

Had he just been about to say he was hoping she was interested in him? Had he, effectively, told her that she only had to say the word and something could happen between them?

'I'll have Bentley,' Iris said.

'Sadly, Bentley's not on the menu. You'll have to discuss that with him. I meant to eat.'

It was clear Archer was trying not to laugh but when he shot another look at Elodie, his eyes twinkled with amusement.

And something more. Elodie just wasn't sure what that was.

Iris winked at him. 'My order still stands. But okay. I'll have the Coq au Vin. I'm told I'll think I've died and gone to heaven. Or something like that.'

'You will. And what about you, Elodie? What would you like?'

'She'd like ...' Iris shrugged and ran two fingers across her mouth as if zipping it shut when Elodie glowered at her as if to say, 'Don't you dare!'

'I'll ... um ... I'll have the smoky sausage casserole with winter root vegetables and horseradish mash, please.'

Her words tumbled out so fast she wasn't sure he had heard them because he was staring at her as if he was waiting for something.

He gave another small cough.

'Good choice. That happens to be one of my favourites.'

'It's as if you two were made for each other,' Iris said, laughing. 'What? Don't glare at me, El. I'm only saying it like it is. Oh. Saved by the bell. That's my phone.' Iris rooted around in her handbag.

'I'll be back shortly,' Archer said. 'Would you like another drink?'

'A bottle of this red, please,' Iris said before Elodie had a chance to speak. 'Where the hell is my damn phone? Ta dah!' She pulled out the phone and answered the call. 'Dad! Finally. Did you get my message?'

Archer nodded and left them to it, and Elodie moved her chair closer as Iris indicated she should, and Iris held the phone between them.

'Where are you, darling?' Frank said. 'It's very noisy and I can hear Christmas songs in the background. Are you in a pub? Or is that a silly question?'

'Yes to both,' Iris said. 'We're in The Bow and Quiver. It's the only pub in the village but so far we're pretty impressed. For several reasons. But I can hardly hear you. It sounds pretty noisy where you are, too'

'We're at the Captain's cocktail party. I'm sorry I didn't call back earlier, but I'd foolishly left my phone behind when we went on our day trip today – which was fabulous by the way. But I'll let your mum tell you all about that later. We were late back and, in my rush, I once again forgot my phone and I left it in the suite for the second time today. Your mum's just been to get it because the battery has died on hers and she wants me to take some photos. That's why I've only just seen you called. Is everything okay? Your message said something about some files you've found.'

'Yes,' Iris said. 'In Stanley's study.'

Elodie nudged her as some of their fellow diners glanced in their direction.

'You might not want to discuss it right now,' Elodie whispered.

Iris glanced around the room and nodded.

'Dad? It's really bad reception and we're just about to have dinner. Can I call you later? I should've tried to call Mum's phone earlier but I didn't think about it.'

'Yes. We're going to a show later and then your mother has insisted we dance the night away, but I'll keep my phone with me, I promise.'

'Great. Speak soon. Have fun, you two. Oh, and El sends her love.'

'And you. And send ours back to Elodie.'

Iris hung up and Elodie moved her chair back to where it had been.

'I don't know why I didn't think to call Mum's phone. Not that it was a matter of life or death. It sounds like they're having a great time. I can't wait to hear what they'll think of the helicopter flight tomorrow.'

'If you live that long. Why on earth did you tell Archer that he's my type? I wanted to murder you.'

Iris shrugged and grinned. 'Because he is. And because we're only here for one more night. You can thank me later. Or tomorrow morning. I'm hoping I'll be busy tonight myself.'

'Iris! They'll think we're a pair of tarts or something.'

'Or free-spirited, independent, forthright women who know what they want and how to get it.'

'Yeah, right. Because that's how all the men we've ever dated have thought of us. Not!'

Chapter 18

Marian was right about Bentley's food. Elodie and Iris tried mouthfuls of one another's and both meals were divine. Although Elodie was glad she's ordered the smoky sausage casserole because in her opinion that just had the edge, perhaps in part because Archer had said it was one of his favourite dishes.

They followed their mains with dessert. Chocolate and clementine Torte, laced with Cointreau and accompanied by a Cointreau cream for Elodie, which Archer had said he was certain she would adore – and she had. Cinnamon spiced warm pear Pavlova with Amaretto ice cream for Iris.

Iris savoured the last mouthful and asked Archer, who was passing their table at that moment, to give their compliments to the chef – and her phone number, she joked. Except Elodie knew Iris wasn't really joking.

'I wish we weren't leaving tomorrow,' Iris added.

Archer laughed. 'Careful what you wish for,' he said, serving her own words back to her. 'Would you like coffee?'

'Irish coffee for me, please,' said Iris.

'I don't suppose you've got hot chocolate, have you?' Elodie asked.

'I have. But sadly not the one you ordered the day we met. Although you can have one with cream and marshmallows and laced with whisky, or bourbon, or rum, or Bailey's. Or, if you're that way inclined, a selection of all those.'

'Just the cream and marshmallows, please. I don't want a hangover again tomorrow, especially as we're driving home in the afternoon.'

'Do you have to? Drive home tomorrow, I mean.'

Elodie saw Iris wink at her with a beaming smile but for a moment she was lost for words. Was he asking her not to?

'I ... er. I suppose not. Except I came with Iris.'

'Oh.' He looked a little embarrassed. 'I meant ... the forecast for tomorrow isn't great. They're saying there's a good chance we'll get snow tonight and that it'll settle. Although with all the rain over the last few days, it might simply turn to slush. Depends how much we get, I suppose. Not that that's the only reason. It would … it would've been nice if I'd had a chance to get to know you. Both of you.' He cleared his throat. 'I'll get your drinks.' With that, he hurried away.

'Ooooooh!' said Iris, fluttering her eyelashes and pumping her clenched hands back and forth from her heart as if it were pounding in her chest. 'Archer wants you to stay.'

'Unfortunately, I think Archer was simply saying we shouldn't drive home in bad weather.'

'Imagine being curled up in front of a fire like the one in here, with thick, fluffy white snow falling outside and Archer's strong arms wrapped around you.' Iris let out a long and swoony sigh.

'Oh shut up. I don't want to imagine something that's never going to happen.'

'Why not? He clearly likes you.'

'Maybe. Maybe not. And believe me, I'd like nothing better. But I can't get that thick red file out of my head.' She leant forward. 'What if he's done something really bad, Iris? What if he's … even worse than Ben?'

'The man who shall not be named, you mean? Is it possible for any man to be worse than him? Don't think so!'

Some of the diners seated near the windows pointed excitedly to outside and Elodie turned to see what the fuss was about.

'It's snowing, Iris! Archer was right.'

Chapter 19

Elodie accompanied Iris when she went outside to phone her dad. They could've found a relatively quiet spot in the pub – like the ladies' loos for example, but both of them wanted to get some fresh air, although mainly, they both wanted to see the snow. It rarely seemed to snow in London these days and even when it did, it never lasted long. The white flakes soon turned to grey slush as the hordes of pedestrians and streams of traffic crushed the sparkle out of it. But here, it somehow seemed even more magical.

It had been snowing for precisely thirty minutes but already the pub garden was carpeted in white, fluffy flakes and the grass, which had a coating of frost before the snow arrived, crunched beneath their feet.

'It's beautiful,' Elodie said.

'It certainly is,' Iris agreed, shivering noticeably in the cold. 'But neither of us will think so tomorrow when we're slipping and sliding down motorways covered in ice.'

She wrapped her coat and scarf tighter around her and called her dad.

'Unless,' Elodie said, 'We don't go back tomorrow. It's not as if either of us really has to. I can deal with anything I need to, from down here and you told me you haven't booked any clients in for tomorrow.'

'We could.' Iris grinned at her. 'Hold that thought. Hi, Dad. Can you talk?'

Iris put her phone on speaker and Elodie glanced around to check no one else was within earshot.

'Hello, darling. Yes. I'll just take you out on deck though.' He chuckled and added, 'Your mum's coming too.'

'Hi, Mum,' Iris said.

'Hello, darling. It's a glorious night here, so warm still with just a slight breeze and the sky is a blanket of stars.'

'It's bloody freezing here. And you'll never believe this, but it's snowing!'

'Snowing!' Frank and Sharon exclaimed in unison.

'Yep. El and I might not go back tomorrow. It depends what the roads are like.'

'You take care,' Frank said. 'Those roads will be icy after all the rain you said you've been having and with snow on top of that, you won't see the black ice underneath.'

'I know, Dad. I'll be careful. I won't drive if I don't think it's safe. Now, about those files we found.'

Iris told her parents what she and Elodie had discovered in the cabinets and that the files were different colours. She also explained how they'd had to search for the keys to the cabinets and desk and that they had been hidden behind a photo.

'There's a laptop too but that's password protected so we're forgetting about that for now. We still haven't looked inside the files yet, mainly because El thinks we should respect people's privacy, and she's also concerned about what might be in them. I agree, but part of me really wants to read them. Anyway. We just wondered if you might be able to shed some light on this little mystery. Do you think it's likely that the files are connected with something Uncle Stanley did for a living? Or do you think he might have kept them for ... let's say, not entirely innocent reasons?'

Frank snorted derisively. 'Knowing Stanley, I'd definitely lean towards the latter. You said the files are different colours? And some are in alphabetical order and then by colour and alphabetical?'

'Yes. As I said, we're working on the assumption that grey is boring and red is bad. Or dangerous. As in the stuff inside is explosive and that person really wouldn't want that information getting out.'

'Hmm. I can see why you'd be thinking along those lines, but I do remember something from when we were younger. When Stanley told me about knowledge being power, he kept the information he'd garnered in order of how valuable it was to him, so perhaps those coloured files relate to how valuable the information was to Stanley, not how good or bad – to use a comparison to the festive season – a person had been.' Frank chuckled before clearing his throat. 'I shouldn't laugh. This probably isn't funny.'

'It isn't,' said Sharon. 'Far from it, knowing Stanley.'

'So what you're saying, Dad, is that the colours relate to a person's value to Stanley, not the seriousness of that person's past deeds, is that right?'

'Yes. I would think so.'

'But ... then surely orange would be the most ... valuable, wouldn't it? Because that's the closest colour file to gold. And gold has the greatest value to most people.'

'Yes,' said Sharon. 'But Stanley wasn't like most people, darling.'

'Your mum's right about that. And now that I think about it, I recall him showing me a book he kept. It was one of those address books with about four address blocks to each page. Stanley had those little round stickers you used to be able to get. And probably still can, but that's irrelevant. Anyway, he would place a sticker beside someone's name relative to how beneficial that person's information was to him. But it wasn't based on gold being the most valuable and so on. It was based on the colours Stanley liked the most. And red was actually Stanley's favourite colour. Of course that might have changed over the years but right up until the time we stopped speaking, red remained his favourite.'

'So would that mean if someone's file was red, Dad, Stanley actually liked that person? Or that the person's information was the most valuable to Stanley?'

'I don't think Stanley ever liked anyone, darling. Not even his family. Which is why I still can't believe the old bugger left everything to me. But I believe it meant how much value it was to him. And remember, that doesn't necessarily mean how destructive that information could be to someone's life. It was all about money and power, for Stanley. So it would probably mean how much money he believed he could get from that person. After all, you can't get blood from a stone. If the person doesn't have any money and can't get access to any, then no matter what Stanley knew, that knowledge wouldn't benefit him financially. Oh. Or it might be something as precious to him as money, like who could help him to become a member of a prestigious and ultra-exclusive club, for example. I remember there was one of those secret society type clubs at school and only a few elite pupils were members. Then one day, Stanley announced he had become a member. We never discovered how he did that.'

'Wow. So ... are you saying that the people with red files are the ones with the most money?'

'I would say so, yes. Or the ones with access to money, or something else that Stanley wanted. But there's really only one way you can find out, darling. And that's by looking at what's in those files. Although I'm not sure I would want to.'

'Well, they now belong to you, Dad. El wants to burn them.'

'I agree with Elodie,' Sharon said, emphatically.

'As do I,' said Frank. 'I don't want anything to do with Stanley's dreadful behaviour. However ... there is one tiny caveat. If Stanley had changed, which I doubt but one never knows. Nothing is impossible, I suppose. Those files could relate to something else. Didn't you say the vicar told you Stanley was in the church choir?'

'I did.'

'Well, I suppose it's possible the files could be connected with something like that. But even as I'm saying it, I'm doubting it. Nevertheless, I think someone needs to look at one of the files, at least, just to be sure that we don't destroy anything we actually shouldn't. Either you can do that, darling. Or you can lock them all back up and they can wait until we get back. Alternatively, you could ask Arthur Cole to look at one. I trust him implicitly.'

'Thanks, Dad. Why don't we all think about it and we'll chat again tomorrow? El and I are freezing out here.'

'You're outside?'

'Yep. The pub was noisy and we wanted some air but now we've had enough and we want to get warm. Love you both. Goodnight.'

'Love you too, darling. And you, Elodie. Goodnight.'

Iris rang off after Elodie had returned their goodnight wishes.

'I'm not sure how much farther that got us, but if Dad is right, I think it gives us even more questions. And ... it would indicate that

Archer is rich. Or valuable to Stanley in some other way. Or both.'

Elodie furrowed her brows in thought. 'Or that he can get his hands on a lot of money.'

'True.' Iris linked her arm through Elodie's. 'Let's get back inside. I can hardly feel my feet right now.'

'We should think about going home. Not to London, I don't mean. To the cottage. If this snow keeps up, walking in these boots might prove difficult.'

Iris glanced down at her own boots, which were the same thigh length boots as Elodie's apart from the colour and were now surrounded by a good half inch or so of snow.

'Or easier. We couldn't walk across the fields because of the mud, but if the water in them is frozen like this grass is, and there's a deep enough covering of snow, we might be able to. I say we go back inside for a bit, and see what the weather does. Besides, it's almost closing time, so we may as well wait until then.'

Elodie rolled her eyes. 'You would. But if we get snowed in here it's your fault. Okay?'

Iris laughed. 'Oh, El. Most people would like nothing better than to get snowed in, in a pub. Especially if there are two very hot guys inside.'

Chapter 20

Snow continued to fall thick and fast all the while they were outside and Elodie soon realised that, even if they made it back to Clementine Cottage, they probably weren't going to be driving back to London on Sunday in any event, whether they wanted to or not. Apart from the likelihood of icy roads and possible snowdrifts, Iris had drunk too much alcohol and would still be over the limit come tomorrow.

'Are we staying for another day then?' Elodie queried as they took their coats off and tossed them on a vacant chair beside the table in the window, at which they now intended to sit.

'I think we should. Don't you? It's foolish to drive home in bad weather when we don't really have to. Plus, if we stay, we can have another drink or two.'

Elodie wasn't at all surprised at that.

'I suppose in that case, I may as well join you. Although I'm still going to take it easy because I can do without another hangover.'

What did surprise her was that quite a few of the people in the pub started wandering outside, some having snowball fights, some building snowmen, some making snow angels and others simply taking photographs. And yet, with all those people treading down the snow, it still looked magical and sparkly.

'I'm nipping to the loo,' Iris said. 'Don't do anything fun without me.'

Elodie grinned and peered through the pub window, watching the people outside.

'Not tempted?'

Archer's voice made her jump and when she turned to look, he was standing so close to the back of her chair that she could smell the subtle aroma of sandalwood in his aftershave.

'Sorry?' She wasn't sure exactly what he was referring to.

'By the snow. Not tempted to do any or all of those things?' He nodded at the crowd of people having a good time.

'Yes. But we've just been out there and it's freezing. Plus, we haven't really got the right footwear.' She pointed at her boots.

He smiled his sexy smile and she felt her heart flutter like one of those snowflakes.

'You're probably right. But from where I'm standing they look pretty good.'

Sitting as she was, her thigh length black leather boots revealed an inch or two of her legs before the rest of her skin was hidden by the hemline of the fitted, scarlet mini dress she'd bought that day. She knew she looked quite good, but as his admiring gaze travelled up and down the entire length of her body before resting on her face, she felt like a million dollars. Every inch of her was tingling. And it wasn't from the cold. Neither was the intense heat that was burning inside her, from the fire a few feet away.

'Thanks,' she said, forcing herself not to grab hold of him and plant a kiss on his gorgeous, sexy, tantalising mouth.

'I've brought you something.' He held up his left hand and smiled.

'An empty wine bottle? Er, thanks.'

Archer laughed. 'Not just an empty wine bottle.' He held up a pad and a pen in his other hand.

'Gosh. You really know how to spoil a girl. Oh wait! It's for the tree.'

He seemed surprised for a second but his smile quickly returned.

'You know about the bottles on the tree?' He placed the bottle and the pad and pen on the table and sat on Iris' now vacant seat.

Elodie nodded. 'Yes. Marian told us all about it. Oh. I mean them. All about the bottles. And the wishes. And the tradition.'

He furrowed his brows. 'Why do I get the feeling you think you've said something you shouldn't have?'

She gave what she hoped was a nonchalant shrug and shook her head. 'I don't know. Because I haven't, have I? I mean the fact that you once wrote a wish in a bottle and tied it to the tree and that since then it's become a tradition and everyone does it, is hardly top secret, is it? And the fact that Marian told us that, and I've repeated it, isn't exactly breaking a confidence or anything.'

His gaze held hers until she looked away.

'Not if that's all it was. I suppose it depends what Marian told you.'

'Just what I said.'

'She didn't tell you what it was I wished for in that very first bottle? Or why?'

'No.' She smiled at him. 'But I'd like to know. What did you wish for Archer? And why?'

'Ah. Now *that is* top secret.'

'I suppose it was something to do with a girl.'

'Why?' he snapped.

'Oh! Er. Sorry. I didn't mean to upset you.'

He shook his head and ran a hand through his hair.

'No. I'm sorry. I didn't mean to snap. It's ... a sore point, that's all. Anyway, if Marian told you about the bottles, you know what you have to do.'

'Hmm. Didn't both you and Iris say earlier that we should be careful what we wish for?'

'You should. And there are some things we can wish for that we know will never come true. But it doesn't stop us wishing. You don't have to if you'd rather not though. It's not obligatory.'

He reached out as if he was about to remove the bottle, pad and pen but she reached out to stop him. Their fingers brushed and it seemed he felt the same bolt of electricity she did because he looked at his hand as if he'd received first degree burns – and then he looked at her as if he were gazing at a magnificent star, like the Star of Bethlehem or something.

'I want ... um.' She was struggling to find her voice and she coughed to clear her throat. 'I want to make a wish.' She stared into his eyes. 'And I know exactly what I'll be wishing for.'

'Me too,' he said. 'Elodie? When I said earlier that I was merely concerned about the weather, that wasn't entirely true. I mean, I was concerned, but that wasn't why I suggested you might want to stay. I …' He blew out a quick sigh. 'I'm making a complete mess of this. It's been so long that I've forgotten how … er … I mean. It's been a while since I've … Oh my God!' He laughed suddenly and shook his head. 'What I'm trying to say, without sounding like an utter prat, is that I like you. Really like you. And I … I wish that you could stay.'

'I wish that too.'

'You do?'

She nodded. 'Definitely.'

'But … you can't, can you? And even if you could, it wouldn't make a difference. If you stayed, I'll want more. Much more. And I can't have that.'

'Why not?'

'For one thing, because you live in London and I live here. I know from experience that long distance relationships don't work.'

'London's hardly a long distance, Archer. It's nothing compared to Perth.'

'Perth?' His entire body tensed visibly. 'What do you know about Perth?'

'Nothing! Er. Just that you found a bottle on the beach in the bay and it had come from Perth.'

'And how would I have known that?'

'Because of the note inside.'

Too late, Elodie realised she'd let the cat out of the bag. Or maybe the note out of the bottle in this scenario.

'So Marian did tell you more than you said.'

'Only that you found a note ... and that the address inside was from someone in Perth ... and that you replied to it. That's all. Honestly. But ... I will admit that I was pretty certain there was more to the story. She didn't tell us anything else though. I ... I just assumed the note was from ... a girl.'

'Why?'

'I don't know. I just did. Am I wrong?'

He didn't reply right away and she wasn't sure he would, but just as she was about to try to coax him further, he sighed as if he had been forced to surrender the information on pain of death.

'No. You're right. Marian didn't say anything else?'

'Nothing. I promise you.'

He relaxed a little but not entirely.

'Okay. I'll have to take your word for that. Not that Marian ...' He let his voice trail off.

'What?' she prompted.

'Nothing. Forget I said it. In fact, perhaps we should forget most of this conversation.'

'Why?'

He shook his head and Elodie could tell the discussion was over.

They sat in silence for a second or two, both looking out of the window, but it began to feel like eternity to Elodie.

'I hope nothing's happened to Iris. She's been in the loo for ages.'

'She's not in the loo.' He looked at Elodie again and smiled wanly. 'She's in the kitchen with Bentley.'

'What? Since when? How did that happen?'

'She asked if I would mind if she personally gave her compliments to the chef and I told her that was fine because we've finished serving and he'd be clearing up.'

'He won't be doing that for long if Iris has her way. Oh! I didn't mean to say that out loud.'

He shrugged and a smile tugged at his mouth. 'We're all adults.'

'Can I make my wish now then? Iris may be a while.'

'Yes, of course.' He stood up. 'I'll come back in a few minutes and help you tie the bottle to the tree.'

'Don't go! I mean ... you don't have to go. I can write my wish with you here.'

He hesitated for a second as if he wasn't sure whether to stay or go but then he smiled, sat down again and slid the pad and pen across the table to her. She wrote her wish, tore off the page and slid the pad and pen back to him. Then she folded the sheet of paper so that her words couldn't be seen and curled the page into a tube shape. He held the neck of the bottle towards her and she slipped her wish inside.

They both got up and she shrugged on her coat and wrapped her scarf around her neck.

'Are you going to get a coat?' she asked.

'Nah. I'll be fine. Coming?' He was already heading for the door.

'You bet. But I need my gloves and I can't ... oh there they are.' She spotted them on the empty seat nearby and, after slipping her hands inside, she followed him out into the bitterly cold and snowy night.

The snow was even heavier now and within minutes, their hair and clothes were covered with large white flakes, some of which clung and didn't seem to want to melt.

'Anywhere in particular you want your bottle to go?'

She smiled. 'I'm tempted to say right at the top just to see if you'd get a ladder out and put it there, but anywhere is fine.'

'I will if you want me to,' he said, and she could tell he meant it.

She shook her head. 'Thanks. But really, anywhere will do. Oh. As long as you promise me you won't read it.'

'I would never do that. Read it, that is. I promise.' He smiled. 'Besides, everyone knows it's bad luck to read someone else's wish.'

'Is it? I didn't know that.'

'You do now.'

'Which bottle is yours?'

She scanned the tree. Maybe she could guess which one it was.

'I haven't hung one yet.'

'Couldn't you decide what to wish for?'

'I know exactly what to wish for. I wish the same thing every year and have since … for a long time.' He met her eyes. 'But perhaps … I'll wish for something else this year.'

They stared into each other's eyes until a snowball whizzed within an inch of Elodie and she screamed, not realising what it was at first.

'You okay?' he asked, with a crooked smile as if he was trying not to laugh.

'Fine. It took me by surprise, that's all.'

'Snowballs can be terrifying.'

She tilted her head to one side. 'Are you making fun of me?'

'No! Er … I'll hang up your wish.'

He took a length of red ribbon from the pocket of his jeans and tied it around the neck of the bottle. He then took out another piece of ribbon and threaded that through a little loop he'd left before tying the rest of it to the highest branch he could reach on the tree, standing on tiptoes. He kept one hand beneath until he was certain the bottle wouldn't slip from the branch and then he turned and smiled at Elodie.

While he'd been hanging her bottle she had bent down and scooped up a handful of snow which she threw at him a second after he turned around. It hit him in the chest and he looked as if the wind had been knocked out of him but as the snowball was soft, that was probably more from surprise.

'Seriously?' he said, looking very serious, until his mouth curved into his sexy smile and amusement flashed across his eyes. 'You're going to regret that, Elodie Abbott.'

'Oh am I, Archer Rhodes?'

He scooped up a huge handful of snow and threw it, but she dodged out of the way and beamed triumphantly.

'Is that the best you can do?'

She regretted teasing him when the next snowball hit its mark and hundreds of icy snowflakes slid beneath her scarf and down her cleavage.

'Was that better?' The smug grin on his face told her he knew exactly what had just happened.

'You throw like a five-year-old,' she quipped.

He raised his brows. 'You really like to live dangerously, don't you?'

His smile vanished as her next missile landed smack bang in his face.

'Does that snow taste nice?' she teased, about to follow that last snowball up with another.

He was at her side in a second and wrapped his arms tightly around her, pinning her arms to her sides so that she couldn't move.

'Truce?' he pleaded, snow still sliding down his chin.

'Never! We fight to the death.'

She struggled frantically to break free, or at least she pretended to. In reality, she wanted to be in his arms forevermore, and as she twisted and turned, she ended up facing him, her body pressed against his as he tightened his hold on her to stop her from escaping.

She could feel his warm breath on her face, and the beat of his heart through the shirt and jumper he wore; smell the scent of that delicious aftershave; see the muscles in his neck tighten and hear the pace of his breathing increase as their bodies seemed to meld into one.

She raised her eyes to his and softly whispered his name and then his mouth was on hers in a kiss as hot as the fires inside the pub, and far more delicious than the scrumptious meal she'd eaten.

She didn't want that kiss to end, but he pulled away from her so suddenly that she fell forward as though she were drunk. Which in a way she was. Drunk on his kiss.

'I didn't mean to do that,' he said, his voice cracking with emotion as he stopped her from falling over.

'I'm glad you did. I'm just sad you stopped.'

An odd smile tugged at that incredible mouth but not for long.

'It won't work, Elodie. I don't know what I've been thinking. There ... there're things you don't know about me. Hell, you know nothing about me.' He ran a hand through his hair. 'This is crazy. How can this be happening? I've never ... I'm sorry. I know I'm not making much sense. I think we should go back inside.'

'She really hurt you, didn't she?'

He had turned to walk away but he stopped and looked back, his gaze locked on her and his eyes filled with so many emotions she couldn't make out what was going on in his mind.

'Yes,' he eventually said, as if they both knew who the 'she' was.

'And you're still not over her?'

'I never will be.'

'Never? That's a long time, Archer. We all think we'll never get over that one special person, but we do. We have to. We can't spend our lives loving someone who doesn't love us back. That's just madness.'

'It's not as simple as that.'

'It never is. And believe me, I'm speaking from experience. I had my heart smashed into a thousand pieces and I thought it'd never heal. But it is. It has.'

He flinched. 'You're lucky.'

'No. I've simply realised I can fall in love again. With someone else. Someone who will, this time, love me back, I hope.'

'It's complicated.'

'Is it? It doesn't have to be.'

He snorted in derision. 'That's easy to say. You don't understand. There're things from my past that ... that'll always be there. And there are things I'm not proud of. I'm not cut out for serious relationships, and I have a feeling that's what this would be. If I let it. And I can't. If I felt less, we could have a fling. Have some fun. But it's already way past that. And *that* is madness. I saw you for the first time yesterday and yet I feel … as if I've known you forever.'

'I feel the same! And why is that mad? Some things are meant to be. I truly believe that. Maybe this is one of them. You and me.'

'There is no *you and me*, Elodie. There can't be.'

'Why not? I don't care about your past. I don't care what you've done. It won't change anything. Relationships are simply about putting our trust and faith and hearts into someone else's hands and hoping they'll cherish us as much as we do them. If we both feel this … bond between us, surely that means something? And who cares if it *is* mad? I don't.'

'I do. I'm sorry, but that's the way it is. The way it has to be. I can't do this. Not now. Not yet. Not ever.'

This time he did walk away. In fact, he almost ran.

Chapter 21

Elodie was still standing exactly where she was when Archer had left her when she saw Iris, running, slipping and sliding towards her. Elodie heard a jumble of words but didn't take any of them in until Iris stood right in front of her and let out an exasperated sigh.

'Did you hear one word I just said?' Iris snapped. 'Wait. Are you okay, El?'

Iris reached out and pulled her into a tight hug as Elodie shook her head.

Elodie wanted to cry but no tears would come. Instead, she sniffed loudly and eased herself away, asking Iris to repeat whatever it was she had said.

'I said that Archer burst into the kitchen and he looked as if he wanted to murder someone. No. Massacre the entire pub would be more apt. And just when things were getting interesting between me and Bentley. Bentley asked me to give them a moment and suggested I might want to come and check on you. What's happened, El? What's going on?'

'I honestly couldn't tell you. We ... Archer and I came out here to hang my wish on the tree.' She snorted a cold laugh. 'Huh! So much for that wish. It definitely won't be coming true!'

'And? What then?'

'We ... we had a snowball fight which he was losing so he came and wrestled with me and the next moment we were kissing and ... oh, Iris! I've never known a kiss like that! Ever. People say they go weak at the knees and we think it's all a load of tosh but it isn't. I was definitely weak at my knees. I was weak everywhere. And yet I felt so wonderful and powerful and ... magical. I thought if I tried I could probably fly higher and faster than Santa's reindeer.'

'But would your nose shine as bright? Sorry. Not the time to make jokes, clearly.'

Even so, Elodie smiled.

'So? Why did the man turn into a raging lunatic?'

'Search me. He said he liked me. Really liked me. And more than liked. He said he felt as if he'd known me forever. He felt exactly as I've been feeling, Iris.'

'What's the problem then? How did it go so wrong? Because it obviously did, didn't it?'

'He just pulled away and said it couldn't happen. Ever. And not just because we live about sixty miles apart. He said there're things in his past. And that I don't know him and ... and ... other stuff that didn't make much sense. And then he stormed off and left me standing here, wondering when the next train was going to hit me.'

'That's weird. Maybe he just needs time to think things through.'

'He seemed pretty certain.'

'Okay. In that case I suppose we might as well go home.'

'To London? Now? In this weather?'

Iris tutted. 'Don't be daft. I meant to the cottage.'

'What about Bentley?'

'What about him?'

'You said things were getting interesting.'

'They were. But that can wait. Bentley's not going anywhere. And nor am I. Apart from home to the cottage with my best friend. And we're going to get drunk, and put up those bloody decorations, and dance around the Christmas tree. Oh wait. We don't have a tree. Apart from the one outside. But I'm not dancing around that in this weather. We'll just dance. We don't need a tree. And now I'm not making any sense either. I think the cold is freezing my brain cells. Let's go.'

'But what about Archer?'

'He knows where we'll be if he has an epiphany.' Iris stepped forward, pulling Elodie with her. 'And I'll tell you what else we're going to do. Or at least, you are. You're going to read his bloody file whether you think it's wrong or not. That way you'll know how bad those things are from his past. He might be doing you a massive favour, El. I mean, he could be really evil or something. He could be wanted by Interpol. He could be an Alien. And I mean from space, not from abroad. Or ... maybe he's really a vampire, or a werewolf.'

Elodie burst out laughing. 'I love you, Iris Talbot. Why is it that you always know how to make me laugh no matter how dire the situation is?'

'It's my superpower. But what makes you think I was joking?'

'Because as much as I'd love it to be otherwise, space aliens, vampires and werewolves simply don't exist.'

'Aha! So you think the Interpol bit might be true?'

Elodie hesitated for a split second and then laughed again.

'No, Iris. I do not!'

They walked on, trying to keep their balance on the icy surface beneath the thick layer of snow, but Elodie glanced back at the pub. It still looked so welcoming. So cosy. So safe, somehow.

Until a thought popped into her head and a phantom knife of ice pierced her heart.

'What ... what if Archer is going to die?'

Iris tutted. 'We're all going to die, El.'

'I know that. I meant what if he's going to die *soon*? You know? From a life-long illness or something else terminal?'

'That's right, El. Look on the bright side. Of course, he's not, you idiot. Don't you think if that were the case the guy would want to live life to the full? To take any chance he could to have sex with a beautiful woman like you?'

Iris had a point. Although Elodie would hardly call herself beautiful.

Chapter 22

'I can't do it, Iris. I won't. It's not right.'

Iris shoved the thick red file across the floor, where they sat crossed legged, opposite one another in Stanley's study, with two large glasses of brandy by their sides.

It had taken them twenty minutes to stagger from the pub to Clementine Cottage, not because they were drunk, but because walking in such weather, especially in high-heeled boots, across snow-covered fields which had more hidden potholes than the roads they had driven down this weekend, was more difficult than either had anticipated.

Not that they had much choice. They stood more chance of winning the Lottery jackpot than they did of getting a cab on a Saturday night in such a small village during a snowstorm.

At least the heating was on when they arrived home. Iris had set it to a constant, balmy twenty-one degrees and a wall of warmth hit them the moment they unlocked the front door.

They'd both changed into their pyjamas and come back downstairs to put up some Christmas decorations. An hour later, every room on the ground floor had been decorated, albeit fairly sparsely, with the fairy lights, garlands, trinkets, ornaments, festive lanterns and Christmas bunting they had bought at the Christmas Market.

Two large Christmas stockings now hung from the mantlepiece in the sitting room which was draped with a garland of holly, mistletoe, pine cones and twinkling lights but the room still looked bare without a Christmas tree and they decided that was something they would have to get, in addition to decorations for the large tree outside.

Once all that was done, they went to take another look at the files in Stanley's study.

'Fine,' Iris said, stretching out one leg and pushing Archer's file even closer towards Elodie, with her foot. 'Whatever. But I honestly think you should. I'll tell you what. Why not take it upstairs to bed with you and sleep on it. Not literally, because that would be uncomfortable, but have it beside your bed and see what your subconscious tells you in your dreams.'

Elodie raised her eyebrows. 'Are you being serious?'

'Yes. Bentley told me this evening that he had a dream a couple of nights ago about a woman singing to him and he asked if they could sing a duet. And tonight he met me. And I'm a voice coach. You see. The power of the subconscious mind.'

'No. I don't see. You mean he had a premonition that he would meet you and you'd sing together?'

Iris tutted. 'No. He had a dream that *told* him he would meet a woman – me – and we would make sweet music together.'

Elodie choked on her brandy. 'Please tell me that wasn't what he said.'

Iris grinned. 'Yeah. It was. Pathetic, right? But he looks good and he smelt good and his cooking is to die for, so I was prepared to overlook the crappy chat up line. And it was all going so well … until Archer stormed in.'

'Sorry I ruined your night.'

'Archer ruined my night, not you. And it was probably a good thing. You'd never have made it back here alone. I would've found you tomorrow, face down in the snow, half eaten by those foxes and pecked at by the robin.'

'Unless Archer had come to my rescue and swept me into his arms and carried me back here. Or back to his place.'

'But isn't this more fun?' Iris laughed.

'Infinitely.' Elodie looked at the file. 'I suppose I could take a quick peek. Just a couple of pages. I definitely can't read it all. But not tonight. I don't think I'm sober enough to take in whatever it says inside. Or to make a decision whether to read any of it or not. I know you think I'm being foolish but if the roles were reversed, I'd hate to think someone I fancied, but who was virtually a stranger, knew every sordid detail of my life. I don't think I'd ever feel entirely comfortable with them.'

'If I'm honest, nor would I. But if I were in your shoes right now, not that you're wearing any, I would still read that bloody file. And if what Dad said is correct, it may not be sordid at all. Archer might know a State secret or something, or the formula to cure ... some dreadful disease. Or the winning Lottery numbers for the next month.'

Elodie grinned before stifling a yawn. 'I know you'd read it if you were me. But you're not, so promise me you won't.'

Iris sighed. 'I promise.'

'Thank you. And on that note, I think I'll go to bed.' She got to her feet. 'I can't believe it's still snowing out there. We might wake up and find we can't open the front door. Pleasant dreams, Iris.'

'Aren't you forgetting something?' Iris pointed at the red file.

Elodie tutted. 'I'll take it with me, just to keep you happy.'

'If you do read any of it, I hope you'll tell me what it says. No secrets, remember? Ever.'

'That was between you and me! I don't think it includes someone else's secrets.'

'Strictly speaking, Stanley, was someone else's secret – my mum and dad's, but you were cross I hadn't told you about him. And you're forgetting, I can read that file anytime I want. But I've just promised I won't. Damn it.' Iris blew her a kiss. 'Sleep well.'

But Elodie couldn't sleep. She tossed and turned for at least an hour, remembering that kiss. What it felt like to be in Archer's arms. Trying to recall every word he said. Trying to forget the look he'd given her when he'd turned and walked away. And all the while, despite the fact it wasn't possible, that damn red file sat on her bedside table flashing brighter than Rudolph's nose.

She must have eventually drifted off but she woke with a start and in a cold sweat.

Someone had screamed.

She remembered it was the fox and she closed her eyes again, her heart racing and adrenaline pumping through her body.

The fox called out again.

And again.

The bloody thing would make a great guard dog. Assuming you could get it to do that at the right time.

She waited for it to stop, or to trot away to somewhere else and disturb someone else's sleep.

Peace and quiet reigned once more and she snuggled further down under the duvet.

Iris was still up. Elodie could hear her moving around downstairs. Perhaps she was also having trouble sleeping.

An image of Archer crept into her head and she half imagined, half dreamed that he was coming to find her. Coming to tell her he was wrong. Coming to take her in his arms and kiss her like he had earlier. Coming to ...

Elodie opened her eyes.

If Iris was downstairs, who was in the room next door, snoring lightly, but snoring nevertheless?

A river of ice ran through her. She could still hear someone moving about below.

And it clearly wasn't Iris.

Unless ... had Iris contacted Bentley and invited him to spend the night? Was he downstairs getting himself a drink, maybe?

There was only one way to find out.

She eased back the duvet and slipped quietly off the bed, taking soft steps towards the door, although she was entirely sure why. If it was Bentley, there was no need for her to creep around, but nevertheless, she did.

A floorboard creaked beneath her feet and she stopped, holding her breath and trying not to panic.

The person downstairs must've stopped too. Only silence drifted up the stairs and along the hall.

Seconds ticked by in her head like a pendulum banging against the sides of her brain, until the person moved again, and so did Elodie, even more carefully than before.

She reached the door which she'd left ajar as she always did at home, and oh so slowly eased it wider open. She looked each way along the hall and saw a flash of light from below; the sort of light from the beam of a torch.

Why would Bentley use a torch? Why not just switch on the lights?

Because it wasn't Bentley, was it?

She already knew that. She felt it with every fibre of her being. Whoever it was downstairs, they didn't want to turn on the lights, and they certainly hadn't been invited.

She gingerly made her way to Iris' room. Luckily, the door was wide open and Elodie could see Iris, sound asleep, lying on her back with one leg hanging over the edge, and her mouth wide open.

Elodie crept forward, thankful that no floorboards creaked in here. She reached out and gently shook Iris who snuffled and grunted like a pig. She shook her again and this time Iris awoke.

'What the–?'

'Shuusshh', Elodie whispered. 'Is Bentley here?' She placed a finger over her mouth to indicate Iris should speak quietly, even though she knew what the answer would be, a small part of her still hoped she might be wrong.

'Bentley?' Iris whispered. 'Of course not. Why are we whispering?'

Elodie felt the colour drain from her like a melting snowman and half expected to see a pool of white surrounding her.

Was white the colour of fear?

And why was she thinking about colours when someone might be about to murder them both?

'Because there's someone moving about downstairs.'

'What?' The look of surprise on Iris' face turned to fear and then very quickly, to anger. 'I'm calling the police,' she said, grabbing her phone and pressing the numbers 999.

'Emergency. Which service?' the operator asked.

'Police,' Iris replied.

'Putting you through.'

Iris put the phone on speaker, jumped out of bed and ran to the door, grabbing Elodie's wrist on the way.

'We've called the police and they're on their way!' Iris yelled into the darkness of the empty hall.

She immediately slammed the door and indicated that Elodie should help her move the chest of drawers in front of it, which they did in a matter of seconds, and as the police operator responded, the sound of footsteps running along the hall downstairs and the front door being opened meant the intruder had left the cottage.

Chapter 23

Despite there being at least a foot of snow throughout the village, and in some places even more, Clementine Cottage was busier on Sunday morning than the Millside Christmas Market. At least it felt that way to Elodie who had yet another headache, this time from lack of sleep, not a hangover.

The police had arrived within minutes, in spite of the weather conditions, blue lights flashing and sirens blaring like some massive out of tune, musical Christmas decoration. Elodie and Iris met them at the door, having moved the chest of drawers back into place in the certain knowledge that the intruder was long gone.

Iris briefly explained the situation, who they were and why they were there, adding that she had no way of knowing whether anything was missing because she had no idea what was there in the first place, other than one or two things and they were still where they had been.

A window at the side of the cottage, opening into the sitting room and partially hidden by the huge pine tree outside, appeared to have been forced open and a pane of glass smashed and when asked why the burglar alarm hadn't been set, Iris and Elodie exchanged glances; they were unaware the cottage had one.

One of the officers kindly, and perhaps rather patronisingly, pointed it out. It was beside the coat rack and currently hidden by their coats.

'I did see that,' said Iris, 'but I completely forgot about it. Besides, we don't know the code and it obviously wasn't switched on when we arrived or it would've gone off when we let ourselves in. The vicar probably turned it off. Or the police who were called when my uncle's body was discovered.'

'So nothing seems to have been stolen?'

'As I explained, I don't know,' Iris repeated. 'Oh wait! The files!'

She shot a look at Elodie and they both raced to Stanley's study.

The cabinet drawers were open and every single drawer was empty.

'The files have gone!' Iris exclaimed. 'The burglar took the files.'

'It would appear the intruder was mainly interested in something in here,' the officer who was right behind them said. 'You mentioned files. What sort of files? Did they contain financial or sensitive information?'

'I ... I don't know,' Iris said. 'We didn't look in them. We only know there were files.'

'The laptop's gone!' Elodie said, pointing at the empty space at the centre of Stanley's desk.

Why hadn't she and Iris checked in here first? The laptop was an obvious choice, although only if the burglar knew Stanley had an office. There were so many other far more valuable items the thief could've taken other than files. In the sitting room alone, where the burglar had entered, there were ornaments and paintings which even Elodie and Iris knew must be worth a lot of money, but none of those were taken. Just the laptop and the files.

But why take a lot of files, which must've been quite heavy?

Unless the intruder knew or at least suspected what those files contained and had broken in specifically to steal them.

'A laptop's missing, you say? Can you describe it?'

Iris frowned. 'It was rectangular and the usual basic grey colour, about this size.' She held her hands approximately twelve inches apart. 'But I didn't really look at it, so I can't tell you the make. It was password protected though.'

'Sadly that won't trouble whoever took it. There's always someone who knows how to get around those. And you can't tell me anything more about the files?'

'No. Only that they were different colours. And there were quite a lot of them. All the drawers had files in them. Wait! The thief would need something to carry them in. I suppose, at a push, they'd fit into a really large holdall. Or maybe two.'

'That explains the tracks in the snow. We wondered what they were especially when you told us that nothing appeared to have been taken, but if a bunch of files were stolen, that makes sense. There were footprints and tracks in the snow that looked as if there may have been some sort of trolley involved.'

'What like a supermarket trolley? Or one of those shopping bags on wheels elderly people sometimes use?' Iris questioned.

'We don't know. The tracks aren't that clear because it was obviously difficult to manoeuvre whatever it was in this heavy snow. But my colleague followed them and they led down to the beach, via the cliff path. They ended at the water's edge, so we assume there was a boat there, moored to the rocks. If a shopping trolley had been used, it might've been pushed into the water, but there's no sign of that. I think we should work on the theory that whatever it was, he, she or they took it with them.'

Chapter 24

Not long after the police departed, Rosie and Wilfred Parker arrived.

What the pair were doing up at 4 a.m. on a Sunday morning was anyone's guess, although Elodie had her suspicions. It would have been easier for two people to carry all those files. But would a vicar and his spinster sister stoop to such nefarious activities? Elodie had no idea.

And the Parkers weren't the only suspects. Marian knew about the files and one of the files had her name on it.

But Elodie couldn't rid herself of the notion that Archer Rhodes was the most likely culprit in the theft of the files and that possibility was like a leaf of prickly holly digging in her side.

'Is everything all right?' Wilfred asked when Iris opened the front door.

'Would you be ringing the doorbell at this time in the morning if you thought it was?'

Iris wasn't at her most welcoming when she'd only had a couple of hours of sleep.

'We're fine, thank you,' Elodie reassured them. 'But we've had a pretty bad fright.'

She had followed Iris to the door, irrationally thinking that the thief had been watching and had seen the police depart and then decided to return. Although why he – or she, would ring the bell, Elodie wasn't sure. She hadn't really thought it through. She was both relieved and surprised to see the Parkers on the doorstep.

'Oh goodness gracious,' Wilfred said. 'I couldn't sleep and I'd got up to make a pot of tea. I'm not exactly as quiet as a church mouse and I woke poor Rosie. We couldn't help but see and hear the police sirens and we had to make sure you were both safe and well. Especially after what happened to dear Stanley. I'm so pleased to see you're both all right, but tell me, my dears, what caused you to call the police?'

'We've been burgled,' Iris said, barring entry with the door half closed.

'Burgled! Oh heavens!'

Wilfred seemed genuinely surprised – Rosie, not so much.

'What was taken?' Rosie asked.

'We're not sure,' Iris said. 'As we told the police, we didn't take an inventory when we arrived, so we don't know what's missing and what isn't.'

Why hadn't she mentioned the files? Elodie caught the look Iris shot her and kept quiet.

'We could help with that,' Wilfred said, stepping forward as if he expected to come in. 'We've been in and out of this cottage many times over the years. We could probably tell if something of value has disappeared.'

'Thanks,' Iris said, standing her ground. 'But not at 4 in the morning. We'll bear that in mind though, once I've discussed this with my dad.'

'Oh,' said Wilfred, seeming a little surprised they hadn't jumped at his offer.

'We'll let you get back to bed then,' Rosie interjected. 'Although I know I wouldn't get a wink of sleep if someone had broken into my cottage and stolen something.'

'Good night,' Iris said, unceremoniously shutting the front door on them.

'That was nice of her, wasn't it?' Elodie said. 'Talk about rubbing salt into the wound. She's right though. I'm not sure I'll be able to sleep.'

'Me neither,' Iris said. 'Don't take this the wrong way because you're definitely not my type, but will you sleep with me?'

Elodie smiled and nodded. 'Yes. And sadly, that's the best offer I've had for a while.'

Iris laughed. 'We could call Archer and Bentley and see if they would come and ... keep us safe.'

Elodie frowned. 'I'm not quite sure how safe we'd be. I can't help thinking that Archer may well have been the one who took those files.'

'What? Why? Oh. Because his was thick and red. And I mean his file.'

Elodie tutted. 'Don't be crude. And yes. Precisely because of that. But I also thought the vicar and Rosie could be suspects. It's rather convenient that Wilfred couldn't sleep and got up to make tea at the exact time we were being burgled. And a boat moored at the beach here would whizz over to Hope Head in a matter of minutes. Well before the police arrived.'

'True. Except the rocky cliff is really steep at Hope Head. Arrow Point, below Archer's pub, is less so.'

'I know.' Elodie let out a sigh. 'That's what worries me.'

'But why would he, or anyone else, take *all* the files?'

'Because if the thief only took the one relating to them, we'd know who it was.'

'True. Of course, there is another possibility. Perhaps the thief knew what was in their own file and when he or she saw all the others, realised they could take over from Stanley.'

'What? Blackmail all the others, you mean?'

'It's a possibility.'

It was. And Elodie had to accept that, once again, Archer might be the most likely suspect. His pub and restaurant were busy last night but it was a Saturday. How busy were they on other nights of the week? Pubs all over the country were closing, especially ones in small villages like Clementine Cove. Perhaps Archer needed money. And hearing about – or possibly already knowing of those files made cash registers ring louder than Christmas bells, in his head.

'We ought to try and get some sleep,' Iris said. 'I've got a feeling Wilfred and Rosie will be back later, hopefully at a decent hour. And once word gets out, which I'm sure it will in a place like this, I expect a few others might come calling.'

Iris had been correct. A stream of people, as long as the queue to visit Santa in his grotto, turned up at Clementine Cottage.

Wilfred and Rosie came first, at precisely 9 a.m. and this time, Iris did let them in.

'I can't stay long,' Wilfred said, 'but I wanted to see if you needed me. I've got a sermon that still needs some work. I've thrown out the one I'd prepared and replaced it with one called, 'Thou shalt not steal'. I was up for most of the night but it's still missing something.'

'Was that a joke?' Elodie asked. The "missing something" bit.'

'Oh no, my dear!' He looked genuinely upset. 'I wouldn't dream of making jokes at such a time. Not that I'm known for my humour.'

Elodie could believe that.

'If only you'd given that sermon last week,' Iris said, somewhat facetiously. 'We don't need you, thanks, so please feel free to go and find your missing piece whenever you want.'

Marian ringing the doorbell stopped further discussion.

'Oh my goodness. I've just heard and I came as soon as I could.' She shot a look at Rosie, so it was fairly certain who had told her. 'Are you all right? It must've been terrifying.'

'We're fine, thanks,' Iris said. 'But we were just about to have breakfast.'

'Oh that's kind, but I've had mine. I wouldn't say no to a cuppa though.'

Elodie stifled a laugh. Iris was doing the opposite of offering breakfast, but clearly Marian had misunderstood.

'I'll put the kettle on,' Elodie said, as Iris rolled her eyes.

Archer and Bentley were the next to arrive, about five minutes later.

'Are you hurt?' Archer asked, getting to his feet the moment Elodie walked in with a tray of mugs, a teapot, coffee pot, jug of milk and a bowl of sugar.

She'd been in the kitchen when he and Bentley had arrived and Iris had taken them to the sitting room. Archer looked concerned, but he also seemed uncomfortable, as if he'd rather be anywhere than standing in Clementine Cottage, making Elodie even more convinced he could very well have been the thief.

'No,' she said, as he took the tray from her and placed it on the coffee table. 'We were shaken up last night but we stayed upstairs and Iris called the police. When we came down, whoever it was, was long gone.'

'So you don't know who it was?'

'No.'

'You didn't see him at all?'

'No. But ... why would you assume it was a man?'

He shrugged, looking even more uncomfortable. 'Aren't most burglars male?' He glanced towards the broken window pane, which Elodie and Iris had covered with a black bin liner and almost an entire roll of parcel tape they'd discovered in a kitchen drawer. 'Besides, that window's quite high up. I can't see a woman climbing through that.'

'Women are perfectly capable of climbing through windows, high or low,' Elodie said, irritated that he would assume women were less agile than men, but mainly angry that he was at the top of the suspect list, and she really didn't want him to be on it at all, especially not at the top.

'Sorry. I didn't mean any offence.'

'Fine. Where were you last night?'

All eyes turned to Archer and one or two people gasped in disbelief.

Archer narrowed his eyes. 'Are you suggesting this might've been me?'

'It might've been anyone,' Elodie said. She hadn't meant to actually accuse him. At least not out loud. 'Rosie and Wilfred saw and heard the sirens because they happened to be awake and in their kitchen. I was ... just wondering if you'd seen anything last night. There's a direct line of sight from your pub to this cottage, and the police believe the thief took the files away in a boat. I thought you might've ... oh!' She'd told everyone in the room that files had been stolen. *The* files. Iris had gasped in surprise too, but the cat was now out of the bag.

'Files?' Marian said, her voice little more than a squeak. 'You mean the files you mentioned yesterday? The ones you were asking about?'

Elodie met Iris' glare, but Iris soon smiled, albeit wanly.

'Yeah,' Iris said. 'The very same. Stanley's laptop was taken too. It's password protected but the police don't think it'll take long for someone to crack it.'

'You didn't mention this last night?' Rosie said. 'You told us you didn't know what had been taken.'

Iris shrugged. 'Didn't I? We were both probably in shock. As you said yourself, Rosie, it's pretty frightening to know that a stranger has broken into your home. Files were the last thing on our minds. More tea, vicar?' She turned to Wilfred and grinned.

Iris' parents weren't so easily distracted when they called half an hour later to thank her for their wonderful surprise of an early morning helicopter flight, but at least it meant Elodie and Iris had an excuse to tell everyone to leave.

'This is my parents,' Iris said, 'and we may be some time. El and I need to discuss the break-in and theft with them. I'm sure you'll understand if we ask you to leave. Hi, Dad. Can you hold on for one second, please? We're just showing out some guests.'

Only Archer didn't seem to want to take the hint.

'Are you sure you're all right, Elodie? That window needs fixing. I'll get some tools and come back and do that. Is half an hour okay?'

She didn't know what to say but thankfully Iris did.

'An hour would be better. Thanks, Archer. See you then. Close the door behind you, please.'

'I'll be back,' he said to Elodie, and she wasn't sure if that were a promise or a threat. 'But you've got my number if you need me.'

Chapter 25

Frank and Sharon had been horrified by the break-in.

'We'll speak to Jill right away,' Frank said, 'and see if she can get us flights home.'

'No, Dad! Don't do that. You and Mum have been looking forward to this trip for months. I knew I shouldn't have told you, but I thought I should in case there is something else missing, other than the files and the laptop. I wondered if Arthur might have an inventory. You know. Either because you were left everything in the will, or because of Stanley's death. I remember when Nan died, you and Mum made a list of everything for probate purposes to work out the inheritance tax or something. Anyway, it was just a thought. But I'm pretty sure it was just the files and the laptop the thief was after.'

'We don't care about any of that, darling. What we care about is you. You and Elodie. Are you sure you're okay?'

'We're fine. And if one more person asks us that, I'll scream.'

'Me too,' said Elodie. 'Honestly, we're good.'

'Stanley brings us nothing but trouble.' Sharon sounded cross.

'That's not quite true, Mum,' Iris chuckled. 'He's just left Dad his entire estate.'

'Which is why you're at the cottage. You wouldn't be there if he hadn't done that.'

'It's a good thing you're both leaving today,' Frank said. 'I'd hate to think of either of you spending one more night in that cottage.'

'Yeah.' Iris coughed. 'About that, Dad. I told you last night that it was snowing, right? And that we might stay on for longer? Well, we are. There're snowdrifts of at least a foot or more and I don't fancy driving anywhere today. Especially as we didn't get much sleep last night. Now, don't go off on one. We've got neighbours ... and new friends, popping in and out and keeping an eye on us. Someone's coming in an hour to fix the window. I'll call a proper glazier tomorrow because it's Sunday and there's no point in paying a massive call-out fee if someone local can fix it. And as I said, the roads are dreadful. We'll be absolutely fine. And if we are in the least bit concerned, we do have somewhere else where I'm pretty sure we could stay. So please don't worry. Enjoy the rest of your holiday and forget about Clementine Cove.'

'How can we do that?' Sharon said. 'Anything could happen.'

'Mum! Believe me. Nothing's going to happen. In fact, I'd say we're safer now than we were before.'

'And how do you work that out?' Frank asked, scepticism oozing from the hands-free speaker.

'Because someone wanted those files and that laptop badly enough to break in. Now they've got them. They won't be coming back. There's nothing left to steal.'

'Apart from all the antiques and pictures and whatnot,' Sharon added.

'Oh yeah. But if they'd wanted those, they would've taken some last night. The police say it looks like the burglars had a trolley.'

'A shopping trolley? Now I've heard everything.'

'We don't know what type of trolley, Mum.'

'Give Arthur a call,' Frank said. 'Not about an inventory, but because he knows a private security firm and can get someone to keep you safe.'

'Dad!' Iris laughed. 'This isn't a TV show. We don't need someone to keep us safe. We did a pretty good job of that ourselves last night. Besides, the village is covered in deep snow, remember? He couldn't get here.'

'Call him,' Frank said. 'Either that or we'll be on the next flight home.'

'Fine,' said Iris. 'He'll be my very next call, I promise. Now go and enjoy yourselves. There really, truly is nothing at all here for you and Mum to worry about. Love you. Goodbye.'

Iris rang off after they'd all said their goodbyes and Elodie waited for her to dial Arthur's number but she slid her phone into the pocket of her black trousers.

'You said you were going to call Arthur,' Elodie reminded her. Iris could be very forgetful sometimes.

Iris grinned. 'No. What I said was that Arthur would be my very next call. Which he will be. Sometime tomorrow.'

Chapter 26

Archer was back within the hour, toolbox in hand.

Elodie opened the door to him and was surprised to see, parked next to Iris' Mini, a gleaming black Land Cruiser, which by the number plate, she could tell was less than six months old. Her theory about him being strapped for cash was clearly way off the mark. Unless the vehicle was leased ... or he had overextended himself to pay for it.

'May I come in?' he asked, an odd look on his face. He was clearly wondering if she intended to let him in, or keep him standing there, without saying a word to him. 'I've come to fix the window as I said I would.'

She stepped aside. 'Yes. Sorry. Nice wheels.'

Nice wheels! What was wrong with her? She never said things like that.

He glanced over his shoulder. 'Thanks. It's worth its weight in gold in weather like this.'

Elodie hung his all-weather jacket on the rack and led the way to the sitting room where Iris was lounging on the sofa, her legs draped over the arms, scrolling on her phone.

'Hi Archer,' she said. 'Is Bentley with you?'

'No, sorry. He's prepping for the lunchtime rush. Sunday is always busy and his roasts are very popular.'

Iris grinned. 'I bet they are. But will people venture out in this weather?'

'Yes. A bit of snow won't stop them.'

'A bit of snow!' Elodie laughed. 'I'd hate to see what you call a lot of snow.'

'You might. There's more forecast tomorrow.'

'Tomorrow!' She was starting to sound like a parrot, repeating Archer's words.

'You're kidding, right?' Iris said.

'No. They're saying we could get the most snow we've had in years. I think you may want to prepare yourselves for a few more days here. If you need anything, just give me a call. Right. I'll get this window fixed.'

He went to the window and placed the toolbox on the floor, laying out what looked like an old sack beneath the window, and a moment later, he was chipping away the putty to remove the remains of the broken glass.

'I'd better call the team and let them know,' Elodie said. 'This isn't great timing, what with my parents being away and this being a busy period for parties, but they'll have to manage without me. At least I can do all the admin from here. What about you, Iris? I know you don't have clients booked for Monday but what about the rest of the week?'

Iris nodded. 'Yeah. I'd better call them. Mind you, if it's as bad at home, then they might cancel anyway.'

'At least it makes it feel more like the build up to Christmas should be,' Elodie said. 'I wonder if we'll have a white Christmas. I suppose we'll have to wait and see. Would you like coffee or tea, Archer? I was about to make some.'

'Coffee would be great. Milk no sugar, please.' He glanced over his shoulder at her and smiled.

'I'll come and find the mince pies we bought,' Iris said, swinging her legs to the floor. 'I'm starving.'

'I'll find them,' Elodie said. 'One of us should stay here.'

Archer's head shot up and he half turned and glared at Elodie, the chisel and hammer still in his hands.

'If you're concerned about me stealing something, don't be. I may be a lot of things but I'm no thief. Stay if you want. I don't care. And forget the coffee. This won't take me long and then you can see me off the premises.'

'Hey!' Elodie glowered at him. She might suspect him of stealing the files and the laptop but she didn't think he'd steal anything else. 'That wasn't at all what I meant. I meant in case you needed a hand. In case you wanted someone to hold your tools while you removed that broken glass. That's what I meant!'

'I'll happily hold your tools, Archer,' Iris said, winking and grinning at him.

'Sorry,' Archer said, visibly relaxing. 'I thought ... well ... what with you asking me where I was earlier and then saying that.' He shrugged. 'Sorry again. I shouldn't have jumped to conclusions.'

'No. You shouldn't. But I'm sorry too. I could've explained that better.'

Iris rolled her eyes. 'You stay here and hold his tools, El. I'll go and make the drinks and find the mince pies.'

'Elodie?' he said, the moment Iris left the room. 'About last night.'

'The burglary?'

Was he going to confess?

'No. About earlier. About ... what happened between us. I ... I'd like to talk to you about it. Try to explain as best as I can.'

'Oh. Er. Okay. Talk.'

He frowned. 'Not now. Iris might come back. Not that I'm really sure what to say. Or even how to say it. Er. What're your plans for this afternoon? Better still. Have you made plans for lunch? I'll treat you and Iris to a Sunday roast. You won't regret it. I can take you with me when I'm done here. Or I can come and get you later. We close at 3 and we can talk then. Iris can chat to Bentley. I don't think she'd object to that.'

Iris would love that. And they would both enjoy a Sunday roast. All they'd had for breakfast was toast and marmalade due to all the comings and goings. Plus she wanted to hear what he had to say.

'That would be ... lovely,' she said, and his smile made her knees melt.

'But ... about the burglary. You said you didn't see anyone. Do the police have no idea at all who it was? No clues? No fingerprints? I suppose whoever it was wore gloves.'

'Probably. And no. The police are "carrying out their investigations" to use their words, but they didn't seem hopeful. I got the feeling it wasn't high on the list of priorities as nothing much was taken and no one was hurt.'

'Which is a massive relief. When I heard what had happened, I was so worried you might've been hurt.'

It couldn't have been him then, could it? He'd have known she and Iris were fine, if it had. Unless he was just saying that to throw her off his track.

'And it was just some files and a laptop?' He glanced around. 'I would think half the stuff in here was worth far more than that.'

'Me too. But then we don't know what was in those files.'

'You ... you didn't look at them? Not even a peek?'

'No. Whether they contained business or personal details, none of it was any business of ours.'

'Why didn't you and Iris want to look? Did you think they held ... sensitive information, or something?'

'Er.' How could she tell him they believed Iris' uncle was a blackmailer? 'We thought they might be related to whatever Stanley did for a living, and we didn't know what that was. Everything was left to Iris' dad so really it was his place to deal with stuff like that, not ours. We just came down to pick up the keys and take a look around. Check nothing needed doing until Iris' parents got back from their trip, and to make sure the place was secure. Which clearly it isn't.'

'If someone wants to get in, they probably will. You can't make anywhere totally burglar-proof. Not unless you have bars at every window and several locks and bolts on every door and cameras and lights everywhere. And who wants to live like that? Of course, turning on the burglar alarm does help.'

'Don't you start. The police made us feel stupid about that.'

'Sorry. I wasn't trying to … Er. We seem to be having a few misunderstandings, don't we?' He gave her another of his gorgeous smiles. 'I admire you for not reading the files. A lot of people would've read them. Or at least one of them just to see what they were and whether they were important or not.'

'I believe in that saying, 'Do as you would be done by'. I wouldn't read someone's diary, either. Anyway, now they're gone, so we'll never know.'

Except they weren't. Not all of them. One wasn't. It was sitting upstairs on her bedside table. Or at least it was. And unbelievably in all the commotion, she'd forgotten it was there. She'd slept in Iris' bed and had only gone back to her own room this morning to shower and get dressed. She hadn't even looked at the bedside table to see if the file was where she'd left it. Which it would be because the thief hadn't gone upstairs. Had he? He might've done when they had locked themselves in Iris' room. But he wouldn't have had the time, would he? Or she? She must stop thinking the thief was male. And that it was Archer.

But if it had been Archer – then he hadn't got the one file he'd really come for.

'I'm back!' Iris declared, carrying a tray bearing mugs and a plate of mince pies and one of shortbread biscuits. 'Mince pie or shortbread, anyone? I could say they're homemade, but I'd be lying.'

Chapter 27

Archer's file was exactly where Elodie had left it. Now she looked at it as though to touch it might kill her. That was ridiculous and she knew it but she couldn't help how she felt.

She'd told Archer that she wanted to come upstairs to get changed into something nicer than jeans and a jumper if they were going for Sunday lunch, but the truth was she wanted to check if the file was still there. She was pretty sure it would be but she still had to check.

How would the thief know there was a file he hadn't got?

Unless the thief was indeed Archer.

Is that why he'd invited them to lunch? To get them out of the cottage so that he would have time to come back and search for it while they were eating? He'd told them the restaurant would be busy and yet he'd been able to give them a table. But he'd done that last night, so that didn't prove anything.

She had to stop thinking he was a thief. A criminal. A liar.

And besides, didn't he say he wanted to talk to her? To try to explain why he'd behaved the way he had. That was why he'd invited them to lunch. Not so that he could come back to the cottage and search for his file.

Nevertheless, she lifted her mattress and stuffed the file beneath it, as far into the centre as she could reach.

She changed into navy blue trousers, the only other blouse she'd brought with her, and a Christmas-themed cardigan. Sighing, she looked at her reflection in the mirror. Why hadn't she brought nicer clothes? Or bought more than two new dresses at Millside. She couldn't wear those again today. She'd worn one for the cocktail party that had been a total let-down, and one for dinner last night. That had been a great success – until the part where Archer had marched off.

But then again, she hadn't expected to meet the love of her life, had she?

'Wait! What?' she said out loud. Had she just thought that? That Archer Rhodes was the love of her life. Had that popped into her head – just like that? 'You're being ridiculous! Pull yourself together, Elodie Abbott!'

She stretched her entire body and held herself rigid.

And then she let out another sigh.

Who was she kidding? She wasn't just thinking he might be the life of her life.

She felt it.

It was as if something deep inside, some primal instinct or something, knew it the moment they met. As if something inside her recognised something inside him and they both knew they had to be together.

Except Archer hadn't quite got that message.

She had never felt like this before. Not even with Ben.

When she looked at Archer – even believing he could be a criminal – she felt drawn to him. Like some gigantic magnet was pulling them together. She was pretty sure he felt it too. Why else would he have kissed her last night? Why else would he have looked so miserable when he said he had to stop? Why did he want to explain? To talk. Unless he felt the same as she did.

As crazy as it might seem, they were somehow meant to be together.

She was absolutely sure of it.

Chapter 28

Clementine Cottage was picture-postcard-perfect as Elodie glanced back at it on the way to Archer's car. Or perhaps that should be Christmas card perfect – because that is precisely what it resembled. The idyllic snow-covered cottage surrounded by fields of snow as soft as cotton wool, and trees, their branches heavy with blankets of white with icicles hanging from them like glistening, crystal ornaments. The rickety wooden fence with a cheery robin perched on one of the posts; the sweep of the bay beyond with its blue-grey water, and a sky heavy with clouds bringing even more snow. And just before they got into Archer's car, the sun had come out and the deep layer of white on the ground glistened and sparkled like a white blanket threaded with silver. Could the place be more perfect?

A trail of diamond-shaped pawprints across the front garden meant one of the foxes had paid a visit, the tracks taking the same path as Elodie and Iris had seen the foxes take on each previous sighting. The robin's tiny tracks, veering this way and that as if the beautiful creature hadn't been sure which way to go this morning before deciding to sit on the fence. Literally. Or at least, the fence post. The tracks it had left looked like tiny arrowheads, appropriately enough, bearing in mind whose car Elodie was about to get in.

Gulls, crows and what looked like a sparrowhawk soared and swooped and glided overhead, each calling out in their own harsh sounding tones. The colourful boats, once again, bobbed in the mirrorlike flat calm water in the bay and Elodie felt at peace. But it was more than that. She felt at home. She felt this place had found its way into her heart and she was pretty sure she would find it hard to leave.

But it wasn't only Clementine Cottage, and also Clementine Cove that had found their way into her heart. Archer Rhodes was there, and she was certain she would find it virtually impossible to leave him. As ridiculous as that seemed.

During the drive from the cottage to the pub, Elodie and Archer had hardly spoken one word between them, but Iris had babbled away about how much she was looking forward to a Christmas lunch, and to seeing Bentley once again.

Elodie had, at Iris' suggestion, sat on the front passenger seat and she had been aware of Archer's gaze flicking in her direction from time to time as if he wished it was just him and her in the car, but she had forced herself to stare out of the passenger window and avoid the enticing look in his eyes.

It was a good thing that Archer knew exactly where he was going because Elodie couldn't make out the roads from the pavements; all were covered in blankets of glistening white.

The Bow and Quiver looked just as welcoming as it had last night; the bottles on the Christmas tree tinkled like glass bells as a chill breeze wafted past moments after Elodie, Iris and Archer stepped out of the car.

Archer had told the truth when he said the place would be busy. It was packed to the rafters, but the table he had given them was once again near the fire and with plenty of room around it so that they didn't feel like Christmas crackers stuffed into a box.

Archer had taken their coats and shown them to their table, but after that, and for at least an hour, Elodie hardly saw him and despite being angry with herself for thinking it, it did cross her mind that he might have driven back to Clementine Cottage as she had suspected earlier that he might.

Sunday lunch was as good as the meals Elodie and Iris had eaten the previous night. They both had Christmas dinners, consisting of turkey, sage and onion and walnut stuffing, mustard baked sausage meat, honey roasted carrots and parsnips, baby sprouts in blue cheese and, of course, roast potatoes, crispy on the outside and as fluffy as freshly fallen snow on the inside. All that was accompanied by a white wine bread sauce and a cranberry, port and clementine sauce and washed down with a bottle of locally produced sparkling wine that could give the finest champagne a run for its money.

When Archer finally came over, he looked a little frazzled.

'I know I said we're always busy in here on Sunday, but this is ridiculous.' He gave a short and not particularly jovial laugh. 'It seems most of the village has come out.' A serious look filled his eyes and he leant closer, placing his hands on the table. 'I'm sorry to tell you this, but you can probably guess what most of them are talking about.'

'The break-in at Clementine Cottage?' Iris queried.

'I'm afraid so.'

'I suppose it's inevitable,' Elodie said. 'Especially in a village.'

'Especially one with a very low crime rate.' Archer raised his brows. 'Everyone's trying to remember the last time something like this happened, and no one can.'

'Does that make us pseudo-celebrities?' Iris asked, laughing. 'The first people to have been burgled in the history of Clementine Cove. Everyone will know who we are and they'll all be talking about us for days or even weeks to come.'

'I hate to break this to you,' Archer said, half grinning, half frowning, 'but everyone already knew who you were and quite a lot of them have done nothing but talk about you since the moment you arrived.' He looked Elodie directly in the eye. 'But not all of it has been bad. Some of it has been quite the opposite.'

'Why would they all be talking about us?' Iris sounded surprised. 'Just because we're strangers? Or is it because of my uncle?'

'A bit of both. But if I'm honest, mainly because of your uncle. I'm sure you've already figured out that Stanley Talbot wasn't on many people's Christmas card list in Clementine Cove.'

'We did get that feeling,' Iris said, grinning.

'Especially at the cocktail party and tree lighting,' added Elodie. 'You ... you looked particularly ... surprised.'

'Yeah. Sorry about that. I was. Stanley and I … didn't exactly … get on.'

'You weren't alone in that,' Iris said. 'My dad and mum didn't get on with him either, and Stanley was my dad's elder brother.'

'Yes. I believe you said there was a rift.'

'A big one.'

'I probably shouldn't say this, but I don't think there'll be many mourners at his funeral. When is it, by the way? No one's said anything about it. Not even Rosie. And that's a first.'

Iris shrugged. 'No idea. Dad did mention that Arthur – that's Arthur Cole, our friend and family solicitor, told him the post mortem had been done and the results showed Stanley had died from natural causes, namely a massive heart attack.' She gave a snort of laughter. 'I think Dad was half expecting to be told that someone had murdered the old bugger. But it appears not. Anyway, Arthur said the body was being released and he'd be contacting Wilfred Parker regarding the funeral service, as per Stanley's wishes. That's all I know at the moment. Apart from that Stanley wanted to be cremated and for a small service to be held in St Mary's in the Wood. From what my dad said, the vicar doesn't expect many mourners either. Mum and Dad won't be going because they're away. I might though. Just out of curiosity. Depending on when it is and whether we're here or back in London. I'm not curious enough to drive all the way back down here just for that.'

'I honestly don't think anyone from here will attend apart from Rosie and, of course, Wilfred, but I do think a few people might be keen to celebrate the fact that Stanley's no longer with us, as awful as that sounds. I'd better get back to work. Can I get you anything else?'

'Just the bill, please,' Elodie said.

He furrowed his brows. 'I told you. This is on me. My treat. Call it ... an early Christmas present.' He grinned at Elodie. 'Or maybe a friendly bribe. There're some sofas in the other bar.' He pointed to a room that Elodie and Iris hadn't yet seen inside. 'Or if you like, you can go upstairs to my place. There's a great view from the sitting room, lots of comfy seating, and a roaring fire. There's also a TV, several shelves of books. And you can help yourself to tea or coffee. Or hot chocolate if you prefer. Or wine. Make yourselves at home until Bentley and I are free.'

'You trust us?' Iris asked, laughing like a hyena and making a point of looking directly at Elodie.

Archer looked at Elodie too. 'I trust you completely.'

'Let's do that then,' Iris said. 'If you're sure you don't mind. There's nothing I like more than sprawling on a comfy sofa on a Sunday afternoon, watching TV. And I don't know if you noticed, but Stanley didn't have one. A TV that is. He had two sofas. And a couple of chairs. And quite a lot of window seats.' She laughed again.

'I think Stanley preferred watching things other than those on TV. Er. Just go through that door behind the bar and there's a flight of stairs on the left. The sitting room is at the front, so turn right at the top of the stairs, but you're welcome to look around. Not too closely though. Dusting and cleaning in general are not my favourite pastimes in the world.'

Chapter 29

Elodie thoroughly enjoyed the fifty minutes or so she had to wait until Archer came to find her so that they could have their 'talk'. And Iris did too but for different reasons.

They had a quick look around the first floor of Archer's private residence, which consisted of a spacious sitting room which led into a smaller but still light and airy dining room and then doubled back into a large kitchen that wouldn't look out of place in one of those cooking shows on TV.

After that, they ascended a second flight of stairs where a hall, which was flooded with light from a glass lantern window in the centre of the ceiling and the roof, led into a pristine bathroom with a walk-in shower the length of one side of the room, and expensively tiled floor and walls. There were three other doors in the hall, each of which opened into fairly plain but expensively decorated bedrooms.

Elodie was particularly eager to see the master bedroom and Iris had to drag her away from that. It wasn't difficult for Elodie to imagine herself and Archer naked in the king-sized bed, wrapped in each other's arms, gazing out of the picture window opposite that had far-reaching views to the lighthouse, the church, the bay and the sea and horizon in the distance.

Returning to the sitting room, Iris switched on the TV and made herself at home on one of the two extremely comfy-looking sofas, while Elodie walked to one of the windows where she sat in an equally comfortable armchair, admiring the vista beyond.

'Your home is beautiful,' Elodie said to Archer later as they walked side by side in the pub garden, navigating their way, with some difficulty in Elodie's case, through the deep but rapidly melting snow. The sun had fought its way through the heavy clouds and had been shining for several hours and although its rays weren't at their strongest at this time of year, it had certainly made an impact. Now though, it was just starting to set and was casting a rainbow of colours across the sky.

'Thanks. I like it,' Archer replied. 'I had it redecorated when I bought the pub from Mum and Dad. I told you I own the place, right?' He laughed heartily and shook his head. 'Why is it that whenever I talk to you, I make myself sound like a total plonker? Next I'll be trying to impress you with my credit score.'

His laughter was infectious.

'You don't! You sound lovely.' She threw him a sidelong glance and grinned. 'But what is your credit score? Just as a matter of interest.'

He laughed even more.

Until Elodie's boot slipped on an icy patch and Archer reached out and grabbed her arm, linking it through his and steadying her, moving closer so that their sides almost touched and their coats brushed against one another.

'This wasn't a brilliant idea, was it?' he said, stopping and twisting round so that he could look her directly in the eye. 'May I suggest driving you to Millside before it closes so that you can buy some more appropriate footwear?'

There was no way she was going shoe shopping with a man. Besides, it was gone 3 and the shops would close at 4, which meant they had less than an hour. That was nowhere near enough time for her to make a decision on new footwear.

'Thanks, but I'm not really in the mood for shopping and Iris would kill me if I went without her. Besides, I thought we were going to talk. Or have you changed your mind?'

'Iris could come too. But if you'd rather not go, that's fine. Although I do think, if you're planning on sticking around for a while, and I really hope you are, you should seriously consider getting a pair of walking boots. And no, I haven't changed my mind. I'm struggling for where to start and what to say though. And I know, before I even begin, I'll sound like an idiot.'

'You won't. And I promise you, Iris and I will buy some walking boots on Monday. For now though, if you don't mind me hanging onto you in a vice-like grip, I'm happy to continue walking. It's so beautiful out here, and even though it's cold, I feel warm.'

'I don't mind at all. In fact, I rather like it.'

Their eyes locked for a moment and she thought he was going to kiss her again. Instead he swivelled round to face forward and Elodie fell into perfect step beside him.

They walked in silence for a few seconds until Archer took in a deep breath, ran his free hand through his hair and smiled nervously, each of them turning their heads to one side so that they could look at one another.

'I honestly don't know where to start,' he said. 'I suppose at the beginning. But at the beginning of what? At how my life became what it was? Or at the moment it became what it is now? What it has the potential to be. At the moment I met you.'

She felt, rather than heard her gasp.

'What … what are you saying, Archer?'

'I … I'm not sure what I'm saying. I thought I knew, or at least had planned, where my life was going. What I had to do. Why I had to do it on my own. Why I avoid relationships. Why I only have meaningless flings. I thought I knew myself. The type of man I am. The type of man I have to be. And yet … when I walked into Cove Café two days ago, everything changed. All that went out the window. Suddenly, I had no idea where my life was going, or what I had to do. But one thing I did know was that I had just met someone very special. Someone who might – no would … if I could let them, play an important part in my future. The problem is, I don't know how to do that. How to let you in.' He gave a snort of laughter. 'I don't even know if you want me to. I don't even know if you like me. But I think you do. I feel it. And I realised I didn't want to be alone anymore. I wanted to be with you. And to be honest, that scared the life out of me. I'm almost thirty-seven, and for twenty-one years, no one, not one person has had any effect on me, but the minute I saw you, it was as if I'd been pulled into an alternate universe. As if I could have a different life … with you.' He laughed slightly hysterically. 'You probably think I'm crazy. *I* think I'm crazy. I *am* crazy. This whole thing is crazy. And yet, in some completely bizarre way it all makes perfect sense. It all feels so right. As if, by some Christmas miracle, nothing that happened before is as important now.' He stopped in his tracks and turned her to face him. 'Or maybe everything that's happened, had to happen to get me here, to where I'm standing now, in front of you.'

Elodie opened her mouth to speak. To tell him she felt the same, but before she had a chance to get so much as one word out, his expression appeared to have changed.

'This is ridiculous. I know that. We've only just met. We've seen one another a total of five times and yet I feel as though I've known you my entire life. And, if you believe in such things, every life before this one. You probably want to run right now. To get as far away as possible from this lunatic standing before you. And you should, Elodie. You should run as far and as far as you can. But I'm hoping you won't. I'm hoping that in some small way, you feel what I feel. Even if it's only a tiny part, I'll take it. When I kissed you yesterday, I felt as if I had wings. That sounds slushy and corny and as if I spend my time watching back-to-back romance films on TV. Which I don't, by the way. But that is truly how I felt. And, at the risk of you thinking I should be locked up and never let out into normal society again, I had to tell you how I felt. How I feel. And to find out if, by some miracle, you feel anything for me. When we kissed I was certain you did. And if you do, I need to tell you about my past. Because there's something that might make you want to walk away, but I needed you to know how I feel about you first. In fact, I had to tell you. It felt like if I didn't, it would burst out of me anyway, and probably at the most inappropriate time and place.'

He blew out a loud breath as if he had to get all that out before he could breathe again properly.

Elodie had tried to take it all in, but it seemed so unbelievable. And yet it wasn't. Because she felt exactly the same the moment she'd first seen him. As if he wasn't a stranger at all, but someone she knew, really knew, like someone she had loved before, throughout the realms of time and space. Which was utter madness. Total an utter insanity. But that was how she felt. And it seemed he felt it too.

She wasn’t sure she could say it in quite the same way. Or even if she wanted to. So instead, she reached up and brushed his cheek with one hand, beamed at him and with her other hand, grabbed the front of his jacket and pulled him closer, standing on tiptoe to kiss him. A kiss which was even longer than Archer’s declaration.

Chapter 30

Elodie had been completely swept away by that kiss, and so it seemed had Archer, and although the first smack on her head did register in her brain as painful, it wasn't until the second or maybe the third that she realised what it was. A hail storm had come out of nowhere and the balls of ice were like cannon balls, pounding down on them.

Archer looked as astonished as Elodie but he took her hand in his and they ran, as fast as Elodie could manage in her 'inappropriate footwear', back to the pub through the snow, all the while being pummelled by pea-sized hailstones. Archer shoved the door open and they tumbled inside, laughing and shrieking – Elodie doing most of the latter.

'I hope that wasn't a sign,' he said, after a moment or two, shaking fragments of ice from his hair and jacket.

‘A sign?’ Elodie queried, pulling seemingly larger clumps of ice from her own hair.

‘That I shouldn’t tell you about my past.’

‘I’m sure it wasn’t.’ Elodie heard Iris and Bentley talking and laughing in the pub kitchen. ‘Perhaps we should find somewhere more private though. But first, if you’ll give me a moment, I need to nip to the loo.’

‘Sure. I’ll wait for you here. Or you could use the bathroom upstairs.’

‘This one’s fine,’ she said.

She was gone for less than five minutes but when she returned to where Archer had been standing, there was no sign of him. She thought, perhaps, he’d gone upstairs but when she tried the door behind the bar, the one she and Iris had used earlier, it was locked.

She banged on the door and called his name but only a slight echo came back. She rang the number Marian had given her for the pub, but from where she stood, she heard the message on the answering machine. She walked and then ran through each of the downstairs rooms as panic seized her, but each one was empty and the only sound she could hear was Iris and Bentley’s laughter.

Archer had disappeared.

Perhaps he'd had second thoughts. Maybe he'd decided he wasn't ready to share the secrets of his past after all.

But that didn't make any sense. Less than twenty minutes ago he'd as good as told her he wanted her to be in his life; a part of his future. Now he'd simply vanished? How could that be? And why?

She had no other choice. She gingerly pushed open the kitchen door and peered around it. Iris was sitting on one of the worktops and Bentley was making something on the stove.

'Sorry to interrupt,' Elodie said, 'but have you seen Archer?'

They both looked surprised.

'Archer?' Bentley asked. 'Wasn't he with you?'

'Yes. But I went to the loo and when I got back he was ... gone.'

'Gone?' Iris queried. 'Gone where?'

Elodie sighed with frustration. 'If I knew that, I wouldn't be asking if you'd seen him. Didn't you hear me calling out for him just now?'

Both Iris and Bentley shook their heads.

'Did he storm off again?' Iris said.

'No! At least ... I don't think so. I don't know. As I said, I was in the loo. But everything was fine, so I don't see why he would've.'

Iris eased herself to the floor and walked towards Elodie.

'Did you … did you have your 'talk'? Perhaps it was something you said. Or he said. Or a misunderstanding.'

'No! We were fine. Everything was going well. He … he told me how he felt about … things and we kissed and … then there was a hailstorm and we ran back to the pub. But we were going to continue talking. And now he's disappeared.'

'He can't have disappeared,' said Bentley. 'He's obviously somewhere. Perhaps he also went to the loo. Have you checked?'

'Er. No.' She hadn't even considered that, for some reason. 'Would you? Check for me, I mean.'

'I can do that.' He turned off the stove and smiled at Iris. 'Don't go anywhere.'

'That was pretty tactless,' Iris said when he was out of earshot. 'What really happened El? Did you have a disagreement?'

'No! We really didn't. Everything was fine. Honestly. Although I think he might have been having second thoughts about telling me about his past. But he said he'd wait for me and I was only gone for a few minutes. When I got back, he simply wasn't there.'

'Well unless he's been abducted by aliens, which we both know he hasn't, he can't have gone far, can he? Have you checked upstairs?'

Elodie nodded. 'I banged on the door but it's locked and he didn't respond.'

'He's not in the loo,' Bentley said, returning to the kitchen with an expression on his face indicating he had more bad news. He glanced at Iris and then back at Elodie. 'I looked out the front and his car's not there. I think he's ... gone somewhere.'

'Gone somewhere?' Elodie couldn't believe what she was hearing. 'How can he have gone somewhere? Just like that? Without telling me. Without saying a word.'

Bentley looked slightly anxious, as if he didn't want to answer that.

'Do you know where he would've gone?' Iris asked him.

Bentley shrugged. 'Not really, no. But he does this sometimes. Especially when ... he's upset. Or needs to think things through. Or he's worried about something. He just goes off without a word.' He smiled suddenly. 'But don't worry. He always comes back. Although ... not always the same day.'

'What?' Elodie and Iris stared at him and then at one another.

'Are you saying he's driven off in a hailstorm and he might not be back today?'

Elodie asked, unable to understand what on earth was going on.

'I honestly don't know. You could always give him a call and ask. But he probably won't answer.'

Elodie turned and ran from the kitchen, tears pricking her eyes.

What was happening? This made no sense. One minute he was declaring his feelings for her. Strong feelings. The next he had done a runner and she had no idea where he was or when he would come back.

Iris came running after her.

'El! Are you okay? Wait for me.'

Elodie stopped and waited. She had no idea where she was running to anyway. She wasn't going outside in that storm. Tears were trickling down her checks, her head was pounding and she felt as if her heart had been split in two. It was crazy to feel like this. Crazy to be so upset. But then this entire weekend so far had been absolutely crazy.

'What is going on, Iris? I really don't understand.'

'Search me,' Iris said. 'Before you came into the kitchen just now, Bentley was telling me he'd never seen Archer like this. "It is as if the man has seen the light", Bentley told me. He said he thought Archer had fallen head over heels in love with you.'

'Really?' Elodie sniffed. 'Bentley really said that?'

Iris nodded. 'He did. And I told him that you felt the same about Archer. From the minute you laid eyes on him. And that even though you thought he was the most likely culprit to have stolen the files, that hadn't changed the way you felt ... Oh. Don't shout at me. I probably shouldn't have said that. It just came out.'

Elodie glared at Iris. 'You ... you said that just before I came into the kitchen? How long before, Iris?'

'Don't look at me like that, El. I didn't mean to say it. Bentley's just so easy to talk to. About ... five minutes or so, I suppose. Maybe a little longer. Does it really matter?'

'Yes, Iris! It matters. It matters a lot. Because now I think I understand why Archer disappeared. He probably heard you telling Bentley that I thought Archer was the person who stole the files! Oh, Iris! How could you!'

'Bugger!' Iris said. 'Do ... do you honestly think he did? I'm so sorry El. I didn't do it on purpose.'

Elodie was furious with Iris, but there was nothing she could do. She knew Iris hadn't done it intentionally.

Even so, why had Iris said those things to Bentley? Bentley was Archer's friend.

Even if Archer hadn't overheard Iris at that moment, Bentley might've told him later. What was Iris thinking?

But that was the problem. Iris didn't think. She just said whatever was in her head. Elodie had lost count of the number of times that Iris had said something she shouldn't have.

But this! This was different. Elodie couldn't help but feel as if Iris had betrayed her. Even unintentionally. And right now, Elodie didn't want to be anywhere near her best friend.

All she could think about was finding Archer and trying to explain. But there was no way she could do that. Not even Bentley knew when the man had gone. She would have to wait until he came back.

But she couldn't sit and wait in the pub. That would drive her crazy. Even more crazy than she already felt.

The hailstorm stopped as abruptly as it began and Elodie made a decision.

'I'm going back to the cottage, Iris ... and ... I'd like to be alone.'

'Alone? Don't be daft, El. I'll come with you. I'm not leaving you alone where you're this upset.'

'No! Please, Iris. I *need* to be alone. I ... I need some time to think.'

'Er. Okay. If you're absolutely sure. But call me if you need me and I'll be there in a flash.' Iris reluctantly handed her the keys. 'I'm truly sorry, El. If Archer's leaving was down to me and my big mouth, I promise you I'll make things right. I'll tell him it was a joke … or something.'

'I don't think he'd find it funny.'

'No. You're right. I remember how he acted earlier when he was fixing the window and you said he shouldn't be left alone. Sorry. Not helpful.'

'No, Iris. Not at all helpful.'

Elodie dialled Archer's number once again, turning away from Iris because she couldn't look at her right now, and sobbing inwardly as Archer's answerphone asked her to leave a message.

'Archer. It's Elodie. I … I think I know why you … you left. But please let me explain. Please call me back. Please don't let this … this misunderstanding come between us. Please, Archer!' The beep cut her pleading short and she rang off, dejected.

'I want to leave him a note,' she said, ignoring Iris' outstretched hand and marching back into the kitchen where she asked Bentley for a pad and pen.

She wrote a note similar to the message she had left on the answerphone and tore off the page, folding it in half.

‘If Archer comes back, will you please ask him to call me? She begged Bentley.

‘Sure thing,’ he said, nodding, but looking as though he’d rather not be involved.

‘Thanks.’

She let the kitchen door swing shut on Iris’ words of concern. She didn’t want to hear anything Iris had to say. She pushed the note under the door leading to Archer’s private accommodation. All she could hope for now was that he would get her messages and give her a chance.

Iris had followed her out and stood in front of her with a pitiful look in her eyes.

‘El! If I could turn the clock back, I would. You know I would. I’m really, truly sorry.’

‘I know you are, Iris. But right now, that doesn’t change a thing. I’ll see you later.’

And with that, Elodie stepped around her and pushed open the front door of the pub, walking out into the encroaching darkness, feeling more alone than she had ever felt in her entire life.

Chapter 31

By the time Elodie reached Clementine Cottage it had started snowing once again but this time she didn't look at the animal tracks in the snow; didn't smile at the sheer beauty of the cottage and the view. She barely noticed the three-quarters-full moon, holding its own in a gap in the clouds, its reflection snaking towards the bobbing sailboats like a silver oil slick on the inky black waters of the bay. She was too wrapped up in her misery.

She opened the front door and went inside, taking off her coat and hanging it on the rack, as if on autopilot. She switched on the lights and made her way upstairs, her legs like lead as she forced herself to take one step after another.

Once inside her bedroom, she collapsed onto the bed and wept, but a few seconds later she jumped off the bed as if it were made of nails.

She lifted the mattress and stared at the file beneath it. The thick red file with Archer Rhodes written on the tab. It was almost as if she had felt it through the layers of foam and springs and whatever else the mattress was made of. A bit like the princess and the pea. Only bigger … and more rectangular in shape.

She could read that file right now. Perhaps it would tell her all she needed to know. Maybe its contents would reveal something dreadful about Archer; something that would make her stop feeling the way she did. But she knew that wasn't possible.

She pulled the file out and hugged it close and then tossed it away from her as if it had tried to rip her heart out.

She stared at it where it had landed near the window and then she turned away and threw herself back onto the bed and cried and cried until she cried herself to sleep even though it was only around 5 p.m. and far too early to go to bed.

Elodie had no idea how long she had slept but the first thing she did when she awoke was check her phone.

There were no messages.

She dragged herself off the bed and trudged down the stairs, gasping in surprise when she saw Iris standing in the kitchen, opening a bottle of red wine.

'Hi,' Iris said, giving Elodie a sheepish smile. 'You left the front door unlocked. How are you feeling?'

'Truthfully? Like killing you might feel quite good right now.'

Iris nodded and filled two large glasses with wine.

'I get that. And I'll apologise every hour of every day for the rest of my life, if it'll help. But you know I didn't do it on purpose, El. You know I would never do anything to hurt you.'

Elodie sighed. 'I know that. But sometimes you need to stop and think, Iris. You can't always just say whatever is in your head. Words have consequences.'

Iris furrowed her brows. 'I thought that was actions, not words. Oops. Sorry. Did it again. Not helpful.' She handed one of the glasses to Elodie and smiled apologetically. 'The thing is, El, I can't help being me. I've always been like this but it's never bothered you before. Or has it? No secrets, remember.'

Elodie took a couple of sips of the wine and closed her eyes for a moment to savour it.

'Sorry about leaving the door unlocked.'

'It's fine. Saved me ringing the bell and disturbing you. But don't change the subject. Has it bothered you before?'

Elodie nodded slowly. 'Sometimes, yes. There're times when I've felt I had to step in and say something to prevent a situation from blowing up. Like this weekend, for example. A few times you've been less than polite and friendly to some people.'

'Have I?'

'Yes. You were rude to the vicar and to Rosie this morning.'

'No I ... Ah. Okay. Maybe I was. But they shouldn't have called round at 4 a.m. in the morning.'

'They came to see if we were all right.'

'They came to be nosy. At least Rosie did.'

'Maybe. But Wilfred came because he was worried. I genuinely believe that.'

'Yeah. Okay. He probably did. And I'll admit I can be quite moody sometimes and I can snap at people. But at least I don't do a disappearing act like some sulky teenager and ... Oh bugger! I've just done it again, haven't I? I'm sorry, El.' She put down her wine glass and smiled. 'From now on I promise I'll try to stop and think before I speak one word.'

Elodie tried not to smile back but even though she felt miserable, and still a little cross with Iris, she couldn't help herself. Iris' smile always had that effect on her. And besides, Iris was right. Archer had behaved like a sulky teenager. He could've stayed and had it out with her. He could've told her how hurt and angry it had made him feel when he heard what Iris had said. Instead he just ran off. Hardly the action you'd expect from a grown man. And Bentley had said that Archer often behaved that way. Well, maybe not often, but he had done it before and more than once.

Elodie gulped down her wine and slid the glass to Iris for a refill, glancing at the clock on the kitchen wall. It was almost 8 p.m. and Archer still hadn't called.

'Friends?' Iris said, a pleading look in her eye.

'Always. As long as you promise me one more thing.'

'Anything.'

'You don't mention Archer again tonight. Or ever, if he doesn't return my messages.'

'That's something I can definitely promise you.'

They clinked glasses to that.

'How did you leave things with Bentley?'

'I said I'd see him tomorrow. We need a Christmas tree for the sitting room and Bentley says we can get one from Jury's

Farm.' Iris grinned. 'It's near Moneymaker Circle apparently. It's a Christmas tree farm but it also houses a donkey sanctuary and there are llamas, and ducks and geese and other animals that you can pet and feed and generally have fun with. I told him we'd want to go. He's got one of those open back trucks so he said he'll be happy to take us tomorrow morning and he'll help us set up the tree back here, before he has to start work at … Er. Before work.'

Elodie stifled a sob. If things had gone differently today, maybe Archer would've gone with them. Perhaps he would've come back to the cottage and helped decorate the tree. But she mustn't think about Archer. She glanced at her phone. He still hadn't called or texted or made any contact at all.

'He'll call you, El. I'm sure he will.'

'Iris!'

'What?'

'I told you to never mention him again. And you promised.'

Iris tutted. 'I didn't mention his name. I thought that was what you meant. Okay. Okay. Okay.' She dragged two fingers across her lips in a sealed gesture.

And to Elodie's surprise, Iris didn't say another word for a good fifteen minutes.

Chapter 32

Jury's Farm was set back from Penny Lane, the last turn off on Moneymaker Circle and was accessed by a rather muddy track, so it was a good thing Elodie and Iris were in Bentley's truck; Iris' Mini would have been stuck in the mud before it got halfway up the driveway.

According to Bentley, the Christmas tree section of the farm had only existed since 1950. Prior to that it had once all been an arable farm, on which Archer's great grandmother had worked as a Land Girl during the second World War, which was how she had met Archer's great grandfather when he was home on leave from the army. They had met in The Bow and Quiver; the pub having been in Archer's family for several generations.

That was a snippet of information Elodie could have done without hearing and she was actually grateful to Iris for once for cutting Bentley off in his prime.

'Boring!' Iris said. 'Tell us about the llamas and the donkeys instead.'

'I don't know much about them,' he confessed. 'The farmer who owned this place passed away and he left it to his niece. She and her partner moved down from London and their dream was to open a shelter for retired or abandoned donkeys. Someone left a couple of llamas tied to the gate one day and it took off from there. Now they've got the donkeys and the llamas but there're also two goats, two pigs, a few rabbits, along with chickens, ducks and geese. They run the Christmas tree farm to fund the upkeep of the animals but they also have open days with llama races and donkey rides for kids and other fun things to bring in more money.'

'I love the sound of it already,' Elodie said. 'I can't see any of the animals though.'

'They'll be in their stables and barns in this weather,' Bentley said. 'And as the Christmas tree farm will be busy today, I don't think we'll be able to see the animals.'

Elodie was disappointed but she understood. It must be difficult to run a place like this and probably extremely important to stick to a schedule.

The Christmas tree part of the farm had been visible from the road long before they had turned onto the muddy drive. Part of it bordered Pound Road and on Saturday, when she and Iris had gone to Millside shopping centre they had commented on how gorgeous the rows of pine trees were, saying how much more beautiful they would look with a covering of snow. Now they had their wish. The hailstorm of yesterday had washed some of the earlier heavy snow from the branches but some had remained and it was snowing again today and had done so on and off on Sunday evening, so the trees now had a fresh blanket of glistening white snow.

'Do we get the snow with the tree?' Iris joked.

'You can have it if you want it,' Bentley said, 'but you'll end up with a puddle of water on the carpet.'

At the gate to the Christmas tree section, stood an inflatable Father Christmas and his reindeer, some of which had deflated slightly after taking a bit of a battering from the hailstones and were looking a little limp. The real donkeys wearing bright red blankets and coats, all trimmed with white, along with fake antlers on their heads and tiny Santa hats made up for that. There were also two cheeky looking llamas dressed the same, and

Elodie squealed like a delighted child when she saw them all.

Small stocking shaped bags of food were for sale and as tempted as Elodie was to get in line with all the not so patiently waiting children, she restrained herself. They were here to get a tree and Bentley was on a tight schedule.

That dampened her festive spirit; not just because she couldn't pet the animals, but because Bentley's schedule had reminded her of Archer. Not that she had forgotten him.

She still hadn't heard from him despite leaving him two more messages last night. She had left another one this morning, shortly after Bentley had arrived at the cottage and informed her, when questioned, that Archer had returned to the pub last night, but he'd hardly said a word, not even when Bentley had passed on her message for him to call her. That meant Archer had also picked up the voice messages on his answerphone and the note she had shoved under his door. And he had ignored each and every one of them. Clearly, Archer was not going to give her a chance to explain.

So much for him having strong feelings for her. If he had any feelings for her at all then he would have returned her calls.

'This one looks perfect,' Iris said. 'What do you think, El?'

Elodie hadn't even realised she had followed Iris and Bentley into the middle of the trees so she was shocked to discover she was surrounded by pines of various shapes and sizes. Only now, as she stood in front of a perfect, pear-shaped tree at least two feet taller than she was, did the waft of fresh pine fill her nostrils. She breathed it in and smiled.

'Yes. It is perfect. And it smells much fresher than the ones we usually get in London.'

'That's because it's still in a field in the open air,' Bentley said.

Elodie gasped. 'We're not going to cut it down, are we?' She couldn't bear the thought of that for some reason.

Bentley laughed. 'Nope. These are all grown in pots which are then planted in the earth. Each year, the ones that remain get replanted into bigger pots until they are too big and then they're planted directly in the ground. All we have to do is dig up the pot. Carefully though. You can still damage the tree – and the pot – if you put your fork in the wrong place.'

Luckily, Bentley seemed to be skilled at the task and less than forty minutes later, twenty of which had been spent choosing a variety of Christmas tree decorations and more lights from the vast selection in Jury's Farm Christmas Barn shop, they had paid for their tree and it was on its way back, along with all the decorations, to Clementine Cottage with them.

Bentley didn't take long to fix the tree into the stand bought for the job, or to string the lights around it from top to bottom. Iris made hot chocolate for the three of them, and then they began hanging the glistening and sparkling baubles. It wasn't long before the tree was dressed and Iris let Elodie do the honours of switching on the lights. Even in daylight the tree looked beautiful and the fire Bentley had made crackled and hissed in the hearth as if it were gasping with delight.

'Right,' Bentley said. 'I'd better get to work. If you want a hand decorating the tree outside, I can come back later.'

'Thanks,' Iris said, 'but El and I can manage. You could drop us off at Millside though, if that's okay. I know it's in the opposite direction but I don't want to drive in this weather and we can't walk far in the snow in the boots and shoes we brought with us. Which is why we need to go to Millside. To get some walking boots, or snow boots, or whatever footwear is best for these conditions.'

'I'll do that,' he said. 'And I would suggest a really good pair of walking boots. The good ones can handle most conditions.'

'Great. Then once we've got them, El and I can walk back. But we might as well do a bit more Christmas shopping and maybe stay and have some lunch.'

'You could come to the pub for lunch. We're not as busy on a Monday. Oh. Er. Maybe not.'

Elodie looked at Iris, a glimmer of hope rising in her heart. 'We could.'

Iris shook her head. 'I don't think that would be wise. Not today. But it's entirely up to you.'

Elodie considered it while they put on their coats.

'No. You're right. Maybe not today. Let's see what happens tomorrow.'

No one spoke during the drive to Millside.

Iris, who was sitting between Elodie and Bentley on the long box seat, seemed preoccupied with something on the sleeve of her coat, not that Elodie could see anything on Iris' sleeve.

Bentley was, quite rightly, concentrating on the roads. With snow coming down thick and fast once again, visibility wasn't great and even the DJs talking between the Christmas songs playing on the radio, were saying how treacherous conditions were and not to venture out unless it was absolutely necessary.

Elodie starting going through how all the scenarios might play out if she and Iris did go to Archer's pub today or tomorrow. But none of them ended well so she gave that up and watched the wipers swishing back and forth tossing snowflakes in the air with every swipe.

Thankfully it only took Bentley a few minutes to drop them at the entrance to Millside and he drove away with a smile that was as relieved as it was friendly.

'Call me,' he said to Iris. 'Or I'll call you. Whatever.'

'Why didn't you want his help this afternoon?' Elodie asked, as she and Iris walked into the shopping centre via the automatic doors.

'It's freezing out there!' Iris said, rubbing her gloveless hands together and sighing as the warmth from the centre wrapped around them like a Christmas blanket. 'I just thought it might be difficult for you having him there again this afternoon.'

Elodie had noticed that Iris had stopped Bentley from mentioning Archer a couple of times that morning and she couldn't help but smile at Iris' thoughtfulness.

'Thanks. That's good of you. But you're forgetting one thing. That's a really big tree.'

'That's true. Maybe I'll call him later. Or perhaps we should leave it until tomorrow. As I said, it's freezing out there.'

'Iris? How long do you think we're going to stay here?'

Iris met her look and shrugged. 'I suppose it depends on the weather. But I've cancelled all my appointments for this week and I don't have any for the week after because that's Christmas week and I'd already planned to give myself some time off then. We can stay for as long as we like. Or we can go as soon as we want. I'm easy either way.'

'Don't you want to stay and spend more time with Bentley?'

Iris smiled. 'He's great. And it goes without saying, he's gorgeous. But having spent some time with him yesterday, and again today, I can tell you he is not the love of my life. He's not even the love of this week. We could have a fling, and if I stay here much longer, we probably will, but it wouldn't make a lot of difference to me if I saw him again or not.'

'Really?'

'Yep. What about you? Do you want to stay? Or would you rather leave as soon as the roads are clear? Not that I'm sure when that'll be. The snow's really coming down again. At this rate I don't think we'll be going anywhere. Look! There's the shoe shop and right next to it is an outdoor pursuits shop, judging by the name. One of those must have some good quality walking boots. I hope they do them in purple.'

Chapter 33

Iris was right about them not going anywhere. The snow kept falling all day Monday and even with the appropriate footwear – which Iris had managed to get in purple; purple and black to be precise, but she was happy – it took her and Elodie almost half an hour to walk home to Clementine Cottage. The wind had picked up and it was blizzard conditions by the time they'd done more shopping and had lunch so the journey home had been a battle.

'I'm not leaving here until the spring,' Iris declared, slamming the front door behind her making the bells on the wreath outside jingle. 'Even penguins would struggle in this.'

'I don't think I've ever seen snow quite like it. Or maybe it's different outside of London.'

'I'm beginning to wish I'd gone to the Caribbean with my mum and dad.'

'I definitely wish I'd gone to Australia with mine. I wouldn't have met ... come to Clementine Cove if I had.'

'Yeah. But Fate decided otherwise.' Iris smiled. 'Perhaps your ceiling falling down was a good thing after all. I'm sure you'll work things out with ... you know who, this week. He's a man. They just need time to wallow and then he'll have forgotten why he was cross. It's women like us who bear a grudge and never forget even the tiniest slight.'

'I don't think calling him a criminal is a tiny slight. And besides, there's still the issue of his past which he never got around to telling me. And then there's that file.'

'Not anymore.'

Elodie nodded. 'Oh yes there is. Have you forgotten I took it upstairs?'

'Oh blimey! Yeah. I had. Is it still there?'

'It was this morning. I threw it across the floor yesterday and it was still under the chair where it landed.'

'You could read it now,' Iris said, as they walked towards the sitting room, packed shopping bags in their hands, after hanging up their coats.

'I could. But I still don't want to.'

'Okay. Then let's put more decorations up. There's nothing much else to do. We should've bought a TV while we were at Millside.'

Elodie laughed. 'We struggled with these bags. A TV would've been impossible.'

'Not in the back of Bentley's truck.'

They spent the afternoon hanging more decorations before curling up on the sofas, in front of the fire which they'd perfected the art of making.

Elodie read one of Stanley's books but Iris didn't want to read so she pestered Elodie until it was agreed they would go and see if Stanley had a pack of playing cards. Having found those, they stayed up until the early hours of Tuesday playing various card games and drinking more red wine.

'I don't think I could live in the country,' Iris said, when they finally went up to bed. 'There's nothing to do. I'd go mad in a month.'

Tuesday wasn't much better. Again it snowed all day but at least the wind had dropped. Elodie suggested they spend the day making gingerbread men and mince pies, after finding all the necessary ingredients in Stanley's cupboards and checking they were all well within date.

Iris wasn't keen at first but she soon got into the spirit of it.

Bentley phoned Iris twice; once on Monday evening and once on Tuesday afternoon. Archer didn't call Elodie at all.

By Wednesday, Elodie was fuming.

'All those things he said were clearly lies. We could be buried alive up here, or freezing cold, or starving, and he doesn't care enough to even pick up his phone and call!'

'Er. Bentley probably would've told him we're fine.'

Elodie couldn't argue with that. But she could argue with Archer. And the more she thought about it the more she wanted to do just that.

At 6 p.m. when Iris asked what they were going to cook that evening Elodie made a decision.

'I think we should go to the pub for dinner this evening,' she said. 'We haven't been out since Monday.'

'But ... it's dark and cold and it's still damn well snowing! Will it ever stop? Couldn't we go for lunch tomorrow? At least it'll be daylight and we can see where we're going.'

'No. We're going tonight. At least I am. You can stay here if you want.'

'And miss all the fun? No way.'

It only took Elodie an hour to get ready. She wanted to look good but she also wanted to get to the pub in case it got too busy and gave Archer an excuse to say he didn't have a table. She knew they were supposed to book, even during the week but she got Iris to call, thirty minutes before they left, to check there were vacant tables.

Bentley said he'd save them one in any case, and he wouldn't mention it to Archer.

'He's been like a bear with a sore head since Sunday,' Bentley had told Iris, who had repeated it to Elodie. 'I think it's a good idea for Elodie to come down here and have it out with him.'

But when they finally reached the pub after trudging through the snow, albeit via the streets and not the fields, Elodie wasn't feeling quite so confident.

'Too late to back out now,' Iris said, shoving her through the door she was holding open. 'Besides, I'm starving.'

Elodie almost fell over but managed to steady herself and once she'd glowered at Iris she looked towards the bar only to see Archer standing staring at her. His mouth was half open, one hand was holding a glass in mid-air while the other held a bottle of red wine, the contents of which he was now pouring onto the floor because he was missing the glass completely.

'I'll take that,' one of his staff said, removing both the glass and the bottle from Archer's hands. Not that Archer seemed to notice. His gaze was still firmly fixed on Elodie.

'We've come for dinner,' Iris said, shoving Elodie closer towards him. 'And I think you and El need to talk, but please don't shoot the messenger. I'm only here for the food.'

Archer suddenly snapped out of his trance-like state.

'I don't think we have anything to talk about. And we're fully booked, I'm sorry.'

Iris raised her eyebrows. 'No you're not. We checked. And besides, we've booked a table.'

He glared at her. 'That doesn't mean you can stay. The owner can choose to throw you out. And that's me.'

'But you won't. Because it's cold and dark and snowing. Oh for goodness sake, Archer. Just listen to what El has to say, will you?'

Elodie hoped the ground would open up and swallow her. She couldn't seem to speak. But at least the pub was half empty so there weren't that many people to witness her embarrassment.

'Fine. Come through here.' He lifted the bar flap and Iris once again shoved Elodie forward.

'Will you stop doing that!' Elodie finally found her voice.

'We'd better go upstairs,' Archer said, his demeanour softening just a fraction.

He led the way and Elodie followed and when he pointed towards the sofa, she sat down.

'There's been a misunderstanding, Archer,' she said.

He stood by the fire and glared at her.

'I don't think there has. I think I understood quite clearly. You believe I'm a criminal and I stole Stanley Talbot's files and his laptop, terrifying the life out of you and Iris in the process. That seems pretty clear to me.'

'But that's the point! I don't believe that!' Elodie jumped to her feet. 'I'll admit I did suspect you. But I suspected everyone. I know it wasn't you though. I feel it in my heart. But even if it was – which it wasn't, it wouldn't change the way I feel about you.'

'Oh really? And how, exactly, do you feel about me? Only you never actually said. I poured my heart out to you and made myself sound like a complete nutter and all you did was kiss me. You didn't say one word about how you felt. I was so happy at the time that it hadn't really registered. And then I heard Iris say that you believed I was the thief who stole the files and that you'd get it out of me one way or another. Was kissing me and making me believe you cared, your way of doing that? Was it all just a pretence? Because I genuinely thought you felt something for me. Something as strong as the way I feel … felt … about you.'

'I do, Archer. I honestly do. And … did you just say, 'feel'? You still care about me? Then why wouldn't you return my calls?'

'Because I didn't want to hear your voice. Or see you ever again. One minute my heart felt as if it had wings and I could fly to the moon and back, the next those wings had been ripped away and my heart crashed and burned. It's been a very, very long time since I've loved someone and been hurt as badly as that. I never wanted to feel that way again.'

'Loved someone? Are you saying you love me, Archer? Because that's how I feel about you. I love you! Truly love you. The reason I didn't say that on Saturday was because I couldn't speak, I was so deliriously happy. And because I wanted to kiss you so badly that I didn't want to delay that with talk. And do you know what? Even if you had stolen the files it wouldn't change my love for you. I love you that much. And yes. I agree with everything you said on Saturday. This is crazy. We've only just met. But it also feels so right. And the last few days have felt so wrong. I love you, Archer Rhodes. I love you with all of my heart. That's how I feel about you. Now how do you feel about me?'

He was in front of her in a second and had pulled her into his arms and was kissing her before she knew what was happening.

But at least she had her answer.

Archer Rhodes loved her. He loved her as deeply as she loved him.

Chapter 34

It was sometime later that Archer said he still needed to tell her about his past.

'It won't change the way I feel, no matter what it is,' she said.

'I hope it won't. I really do. But I need you to know it all before we take this any further.'

'Before we make mad, passionate love, you mean?'

He raised his brows and then his smile was so incredibly sexy that for a second Elodie thought that would be happening sooner than she expected. But he let out a heartfelt moan and ran a hand through his hair and his voice cracked with emotion when he spoke.

'Definitely before we do that.' And then he smiled again and pulled her closer for a moment and kissed her. 'So I'll talk fast.'

'And I won't interrupt you.' She beamed back at him.

He led her to the sofa she'd vacated and they sat down beside each other, turning slightly on the seat cushions so that they were facing one another.

'Okay,' he said, after taking a deep breath. 'When I was ten, I found a bottle on the beach in the bay. I could see there was something inside and I went into the water and grabbed it. It was a screw top, not a cork and when I opened it there was a plastic bag squeezed inside and in that was a note. A handwritten note. I could tell it was from a kid. Maybe someone around my age. It said simply, "Hi. My name is Wendy and I live in Perth in Australia. I wanted to see how far this bottle would travel so if you find it, please send me a letter and tell me where you are in the world and what the date is." It was dated and I found it six months after it had been sent. I replied to the address Wendy had given and we started writing to one another, and later, emailing and then finally, telephoning. Then, when I was sixteen, Wendy and her family came over to stay with relatives and we met up in London, where they were staying. Wendy was two years older than me but that didn't matter. I was in love. Madly in love. But it had happened slowly. I'd fallen in love with her through our letters, emails, texts and calls. While she was in London, we saw each other every chance we got. And then she went home. I was heartbroken but I was determined to save up and go and see her in Perth. I even considered emigrating. And then, I still remember that conversation as if it were yesterday, she told me she was pregnant and that I was the father. Which I didn't doubt for a second.'

Elodie gasped at that. She had no idea why that had been such a surprise, but it had.

'You're surprised? Upset?'

He was worried. She could see it in his eyes.

She shook her head. 'A little surprised, perhaps. But these things happen.'

Now who sounded like an idiot?

He sucked in a breath and continued: 'That made me even more determined to go to Perth, and we made plans. Crazy plans. But we didn't get a chance to act on them. Four months later, when she was seven months' pregnant, I got a letter from her telling me that it was over between us and that she had lied. The baby wasn't mine and she couldn't continue deceiving me.'

'What?' Elodie shrieked. 'Sorry. Please continue.'

'He took another deep breath. 'I was sure the baby was mine and that for some reason, this was the lie. I thought, perhaps, her parents had made her say that. Made her end things. They had high hopes for her – until she had met me. Anyway, I begged, borrowed and did everything I could to get the money together to go and see her and talk to her. But I didn't steal, in case you're wondering.'

Elodie shook her head.

He smiled and went on, 'I sent Wendy letters and emails and texts, and I tried to call but she wouldn't speak to me, or write back, or respond in any way. I sent her an email telling her I was going out to see her and was about to book my flight. The very next day, Mum and Dad got a call from Wendy's parents, completely out of the blue, to say that there had been complications and that Wendy ... had died.'

'Oh, Archer! I'm so sorry. You must've been devastated.'

'I was. Completely. They told my parents the baby had been delivered but wasn't expected to survive. And then they wrote saying the baby wasn't mine in any event and that I shouldn't try to contact them. Just like that. As if I were a bug they could wipe from their windscreen with just the flick of a switch. I don't know what happened after that. I lost it completely for a time. Went completely off the rails. Did all sorts of things I shouldn't have. Said things I shouldn't have said. Hurt people I definitely shouldn't have hurt. Not physically, but with bitter, angry words.'

His expression darkened as anger swept across his face.

'That's awful, Archer. Some people can be cruel.'

He nodded. 'I thought they were dreadful people, but I suppose they thought they were doing what they felt was right. Mum and Dad said it was for the best and I should deal with my grief over losing Wendy and try to move on with my life. They told me I would get over it. I was young and I had my life ahead of me. But it wasn't as simple as that. I was convinced the child was mine. And I was certain my child was alive. The problem was, I couldn't prove it. I wasn't named on the birth certificate and I wasn't shown a death certificate. When I finally pulled myself together enough to make it to Perth, Wendy's family had gone. Moved on and no one seemed to know where. Or if they did, they weren't telling me. I worked my way around the country and everywhere I went, I searched, but I never found her parents or the child. Eventually, I came home here and tried to move on, but I couldn't. Relationships didn't interest me. Nothing did. All I could think about was Wendy and our child. And all I did was work. When I got older, I hired someone to try to find out what happened and if my child was alive, but all I discovered was that Wendy had passed away, just as her parents had said and that, eight months later, her parents had died in a car crash in which there was no mention of a child. The child had basically disappeared and the trail was completely cold. Mum and Dad persuaded me to give up. And for good or bad, I finally did. I have no idea if that child is alive or dead. If he or she is mine. No clue where the child is. Not that 'child' is the right word. He or she would be around twenty now. But although I gave up looking, I couldn't give up feeling that, somewhere out there, my flesh and blood was walking around and didn't know I existed. And it's eaten away at me for all these years. I can't stop feeling that I let Wendy down. Let out child down. That I failed somehow.'

'How can you think that, Archer! From what you've just told me you did everything you could, and much more than most men would've done. You can't feel guilty and you can't blame yourself. But what I don't understand is why you feel this stops you from having a relationship. Or why you feel that you've done something so unforgiveable that you don't deserve to have love and be loved. Because that is how you feel, isn't it?'

He nodded slowly. 'I'm a thirty-seven-year-old man stuck in the mind and heart of a sixteen-year-old kid. A kid who feels he let down everyone who loved him and needed him.'

'You didn't. You did your best. Your very best. Sometimes that doesn't work out, not because our best isn't good enough but because it just wasn't meant to be. You need to find a way to forgive yourself, Archer. Not forget. You'll never forget. But to forgive yourself and yes, move on.'

He looked her in the eye. 'That's easier said than done. At least I thought it was. Until I met you. In the space of just a few days, you've turned my world upside down. Everything I thought I believed seems wrong. Everything I felt was impossible seems possible. I thought I'd never fall in love again. The moment I saw you I knew I could. Felt it with a certainty I've never felt before. It was as if some miserable, ghostly form inside of me was ripped out, with just one look from you, and replaced with an optimistic soul wanting nothing more than to be happy. And to be happy with you. I told you it was crazy.'

'It's not crazy at all. Not even a tiny bit. It's Christmas, Archer. And Christmas is a time for miracles.'

'And ... and the fact that I might have a child, well, a grown up, out there somewhere doesn't change things?'

'No. Why should it?'

'It might for some people.'

'Not for me.'

It didn't. But what it did do was make her think. If this was Archer's deep dark secret, then why was his file so thick? And what did Stanley hope to get out of him? Because having a child was hardly a crime, or anything to be ashamed of.

Chapter 35

Elodie wasn't sure what her future might hold, but she was sure of one thing – Archer would be in it. She was also certain that this Christmas was going to be the best Christmas she had ever had. Sadly, she was soon proved wrong on the second point.

'We can't get home, sweetheart! We've tried everything. But it's no good.' Her mum sounded as if she and Elodie's dad were trapped in a war zone, not in sunny Melbourne. 'It's because of the atrocious weather that's swept across the UK. Flights are being cancelled left, right and centre. Most of the airports are closed. It's even being reported on the hour every hour on the news out here. This is the worst snow storm to hit the UK since records began. And it's only going to get worse, they're saying. We ... we may not make it home until after the New Year! I'm so, so sorry sweetheart. You're going to have to spend Christmas without us!'

'It's okay, Mum! Don't cry. I'll be fine. I'm with Iris. I'll miss you and Dad, of course, but it's hardly the end of the world. We can celebrate Christmas when you and Dad get back. You see! That makes it better, doesn't it? And it gives us all something to look forward to in January. Honestly, Mum, I'm fine. In fact, I'm better than fine. I think I've fallen in love. No. I know I've fallen in love.'

'In love! How can you be in love? You weren't even dating anyone when we left and we've only been gone for three weeks! Or is it four? I'm so upset I can't think straight. Not that that's important. Are you really in love? Who with? Anyone we know? Where did you meet? What's his name? What does he do for a living? Is he single this time? Of course, he is. Silly me. You'd never fall for that again. Come on then sweetheart! What are you waiting for? Tell me all about him.'

Elodie laughed. 'I'm waiting for you to stop talking, so that I can do exactly that.'

When she finally did, her parents and her sister seemed thrilled and said they couldn't wait to meet him.

'We'll have to get together over Christmas via Skype.'

'Er. Can we leave that until later, Mum? It's early days and although he feels the same about me, I don't want to scare him off by introducing him to my entire family. Besides, we've got a few crinkles to iron out.'

'Crinkles? What sort of crinkles? Not like Ben, I hope. Is he divorced? Does he have a mad ex-wife? You read about this sort of thing in the papers.'

'He's single. And believe me, he's nothing like Ben.'

'Single? At thirty-seven? What's wrong with him?'

'Nothing's wrong with him. And you seem to be forgetting I'm thirty-five and single. Are you suggesting there's something wrong with me?'

'Only your taste in men, sweetheart. So I sincerely hope this one is different. But it's not the same for men and women. Women can cope on their own. Men can't. It's a well-known fact. A man without a woman in his life is like a car without a brake. Completely out of control.'

'Yes, Mum. I think there're a lot of single men who'll disagree with you.'

'Of course they will. But only because they don't have a woman in their lives to show them the error of their ways. What did you say his name was again? I think I missed that.'

'Archer. Archer Rhodes.'

'Archer Rhodes. Oh yes. Hmm. That's got a nice ring to it. Let's hope it won't be long until you get a ring from him.'

'And on that note, Mum. I've got places to go and people to see.'

'Wait, sweetheart! There's one more thing. We might as well close the business temporarily. It's pointless taking orders we'll never be able to fulfil. We can't get deliveries sent out if the weather is as bad as it seems to be. I'll give the team a call and tell them to wind things down. We'll post a notice on the website telling everyone that due to the adverse weather conditions we won't be taking orders now until after the New Year.'

'But it's our busiest time, Mum! This is the party season.'

'Yes, I know. But no one will be going to any parties if they can't get from A to B, will they? And missing one season won't hurt us. Besides, you're stuck in Clementine Cove. You may as well take a holiday and enjoy yourself. Forget about the business, sweetheart. You concentrate on the wonderful new man in your life.'

'Okay, Mum. I will. Thanks for that. And once again, please don't worry about Christmas. Hopefully, I'll be spending it with Archer and maybe with Iris, if she can't make it back to London. I'll videocall you all to say hello. And you'll be home before we know it.'

'And then we *will* meet Archer Rhodes. I do like the sound of his name. Elodie Rhodes. Oh my! That has a lovely ring to it.'

Chapter 36

Attending a funeral on Christmas Eve wasn't really Elodie's idea of fun. Nor Iris' for that matter, but they agreed that it was the right thing to do because, bearing in mind no one seemed to like Stanley apart from Rosie and the vicar, it would be a rather sad event. Even someone as unpleasant as Stanley Talbot should have at least one relative at his send-off. Archer had offered to go with Elodie, despite not liking Stanley, but she had told him it was fine. There was no need for him to go. She'd laughed when he'd looked relieved.

To their surprise though, it wasn't just Rosie seated in the pews inside St Mary's in the Wood. Arthur Cole was there and one other mourner. Not that Elodie, Iris, or Arthur were actually mourning Stanley' passing.

Rosie looked suitably sad, as if she had that expression down to a fine art. Wilfred was conducting the service so he looked respectful. Arthur looked pleased to see Elodie and Iris but the other mourner, dressed expensively from head to toe in black, including a black veil hiding her identity seemed to be genuinely upset. Her shoulders were shaking as if she were sobbing and her veiled head was bowed. Her fingers were clenched as she knelt in prayer, seemingly oblivious to the other people in the church.

'Hi Arthur,' Iris said as he approached, his shoes softly tapping on the tiled floor. 'How did you get here in this snow?'

'Lovely to see you both,' Arthur said. 'You're looking well. The sea air clearly agrees with you. I'm friends with the Judge family. They own Judge's Farm ... at the top of the village ... near Moneymaker Circle.'

He had obviously elaborated as it was clear that Elodie and Iris had no idea where Judge's Farm was. It turned out it was directly opposite Jury's Farm and Iris naturally felt she had to comment on that.

'The Judges and the Jurys opposite one another. Nothing even remotely funny about that. But I'm sure I'll think of something.'

Arthur smiled. 'The roads outside of the village are still fairly hazardous but I felt I should be here, so Lionel Judge came and met me in his Land Rover. That thing can get through snowdrifts as tall as a house. Well, maybe not a house, but it got me here and that's the main thing. Sadly, Lionel ... didn't like Stanley and he wouldn't stay, but he will be coming back to pick me up whenever I need him to. It's such a shame your parents couldn't get home for this.'

'I don't think they feel that way. The temperature's in the low 30s in the Caribbean and it's more like minus 30 here. Well, minus 3, perhaps. But they are disappointed they won't get back tomorrow. They were due to arrive really early in the morning, but that won't be happening now because all the airports are closed due to this snow. Which is why I'll be spending Christmas at Clementine Cottage, along with Elodie and Archer and a rather good chef called Bentley. Hopefully they'll be back in plenty of time for New Year's Eve.'

'Yes,' Arthur said. 'There'll be a lot of families who won't get to share this Christmas with their loved ones. But Christmas is in our hearts, as my mother always said, God rest her soul, and they can celebrate together once the snow has cleared.'

'Aw. That's a lovely saying. Christmas is in our hearts. I like that. And speaking of hearts, do you know who that woman is?' Iris pointed in the woman's direction. 'She looks genuinely upset. As if she actually liked my uncle and this is breaking her heart.'

'No. I've never seen her before. But I do know one thing. Your family was surprised when I told Frank that Stanley had left him everything.'

'That's the understatement of the year!'

Arthur nodded. 'I was equally surprised when he contacted me after so many years. And when he told me he wanted to make a new will and leave everything to Frank, I was as astonished as you all were. He swore me to secrecy. Not that he had to, of course. I could never divulge one client's business to another client, no matter what the relationship was, or whether or not one of them was a friend and the other one was not. But I digress. I asked him why the sudden change of heart and he said a very strange thing. He said, "My heart's no longer my own, Arthur. Love changes us all. I'm told that no matter how black a heart may be, there's always room for light, and if we let it, that light can turn the blackest heart to gold." I thought he was talking about wealth, but now I'm not so sure. There's something about that woman that makes me think she was more than just someone who liked Stanley. More than just a friend.'

'You mean you think my uncle might've fallen in love!'

Elodie was as stunned as Iris clearly was.

'It's merely a guess. I have no evidence other than his strange words, the fact he changed his will in favour of your father, and what my eyes see here.' He nodded towards the woman.

'But ... if he was in love with her,' Elodie questioned, 'then why wouldn't he leave everything to her instead of Frank?'

'Good point,' said Iris.

'I have no idea,' said Arthur.

'I suppose we could simply go and ask her how she knew Stanley,' Elodie suggested.

But the music began and Wilfred appeared and asked everyone to take their seats. All five people, that is.

'Brilliant idea,' Iris said. 'We'll do that the minute this thing is over.'

The service was brief, apparently as Stanley had wanted, but the attendees got an even bigger surprise when Wilfred read out a short letter that Stanley had written himself. It was almost as if Stanley had known he didn't have long to live.

Wilfred repeated almost verbatim the words Arthur had said merely minutes before.

'I have not been a good man, nor even a nice man, for the majority of my life. I don't know what makes us who we are and why I was so cruel and evil and unkind and yet my brother Frank was the complete opposite of me. Perhaps it was a fault in my genes. But this I do know. We do not have to be who we have been, for our entire lives. We can change if we are determined enough to do so. If we have a reason strong enough to make us want to. Love can change us all. I was told that no matter how black a heart may be, there's always room for light, and if we let it, that light can turn the blackest heart to gold. I didn't believe it at first, but I quickly discovered it's true. My heart is no longer my own, and every ounce of the blackest black has been replaced by the brightest gold. Sadly though, it seems that my heart has been black for too long and although I feel more alive now than I have ever felt in my entire life, my heart is weak. I can only apologise for the pain and sadness and grief I've caused, and hope that I can live for a few more years to at least enjoy the light and love I've been given. For this I only have one person to thank and I know that she will be here at my funeral, shedding genuine tears for me. But I hope this day is a long way off. My heart is entirely yours, my darling. All my love, Stanley.'

'Bloody hell,' Iris whispered.

'I think our assumptions were correct,' said Arthur.

'That poor woman must be heartbroken,' Elodie said, wiping away a tear.

'We need to talk to her,' Iris said. 'Don't let her slip away after the service.'

But they were in for yet another surprise. The woman didn't try to slip away.

Once Stanley's coffin had disappeared, the woman held herself straight and got up as if it took an enormous effort to do so, and walked directly towards them, albeit unsteadily as if she were shattered by her grief. She lifted her veil to reveal a beautiful face, around the age of fifty Elodie guessed, but she might have aged well and be older.

'Hello,' she said, in a voice that sounded as if she regularly had tea with The Queen. 'My name is Hermione Dunmore, and I believe we need to talk. I'm delighted to meet you, Iris. Your resemblance to Stanley is undeniable. And I can tell at once that you have a heart of gold. Perhaps not always as bright as it could be, but I can't see a trace of black in you.'

'Er ... thanks,' Iris said, clearly unsure whether that was a backhanded compliment. 'It's good to meet you too. How, exactly, did you know my uncle? We're assuming you were the woman who changed him. The woman he gave his heart to.'

She smiled beneath her sadness. 'I am. We loved one another. But I won't beat around the bush. I'm well aware of what your family thought of Stanley and neither he nor I blame you at all for that. He and I met when he tried to blackmail me. I won't share those details.' There was sincere affection in her smile. 'I wasn't always golden-hearted myself. But my husband made me realise the error of my ways, and love truly does conquer all. Even after his death, I remained a changed person. That is how I knew it was possible for Stanley to change his ways. And when we fell in love, that's exactly what he did. I'm an extremely wealthy woman, so I had no need of his money. We discussed how making this gesture in favour of your father would show how much Stanley had changed. We both hoped he would have longer, time to possibly try to build bridges with your father, but sadly it wasn't to be.'

'Had he really changed that much?' Iris queried. 'We have reason to believe otherwise.'

'You're referring to the files.'

It was as if the woman could read their minds. Elodie was thinking about the files and she knew Iris was too. Arthur may or may not have been, but that didn't matter.

Even so, Iris sounded surprised. 'You knew about the files?'

It was a question but it sounded more like a statement.

'I did. I do.'

Iris furrowed her brows. 'You know they've gone missing? That they've been stolen?'

'I know they are no longer in the cabinets in Stanley's study, yes. And neither is his laptop on his desk.'

Elodie stared at her. 'That almost sounds as if you know where they are. And maybe, even who stole them.'

'Stole is such an unpleasant word. I believe those files are where they should be, but I can truthfully say I do not know exactly where that is, at this precise moment.'

She glanced at her eye-wateringly expensive Omega watch; one that Elodie had seen in a magazine and told Iris she would buy one day if she were ever rich. It was almost £17,000. – for a watch!

'That definitely sounds as if you know who took them,' Iris said. 'And I'm not sure if that's a good or bad thing.'

Hermione smiled again. 'I believe it's a good thing. I hope you weren't too frightened. It was not good timing, I'll admit. But although I knew of Stanley's condition, his death still came as a shock and it took several days before I gave the files another thought. I had no way of knowing what might happen to those files, after Stanley's passing. But I did know what he had intended to do with them. I wanted to be certain that his wishes were complied with. And I am a firm believer in the adage, if one wants something done properly, one must do it one's self.'

'Are you saying *you* stole those files? That *you* broke into the cottage and wheeled those files down to the bay?' Iris's voice was shrill with disbelief.

'Ah. No. I'm more of a leader than an action woman. A Commander in Chief, if you will. And surely you cannot believe that I could climb into a cottage through a tiny little window? But I do know people who could. I can also say this. Today is Christmas Eve and there is nothing more wonderful than discovering a surprise gift beneath one's Christmas tree. Although in this scenario, it would be more accurate to say, a surprise, festively wrapped gift will be handed to several of the residents of Clementine Cove today, by a courier from a delivery service company I happen to own.'

'You ... you're giving the files to each of the people named on all of them!' Elodie exclaimed.

Hermione smiled. 'With the compliments of the season and good wishes for a happy New Year from Stanley Talbot.'

Chapter 37

Hermione Dunmore had made Elodie think. Giving the files to the people whose names were on them, whatever they might contain – good or bad or something in between, was the right thing to do. And Christmas was the perfect time to do it.

But there was one file that Hermione wouldn't be returning because there was one file she didn't have. The one with Archer Rhodes written on the tab.

Elodie still hadn't looked inside, despite being tempted to do so.

He'd told her about his child. He'd told her how he'd felt. He'd told her things he hadn't told anyone else before. He'd told her he'd gone off the rails and completely lost the plot. He'd told her he'd said and done things he regretted. Perhaps some of those things were bad. Very bad. But she couldn't believe they were. A man who made her feel this good couldn't possibly be that bad.

And even if he had been bad in his past, did that matter now? People went to prison and came out completely reformed. And Archer hadn't been to prison. He'd never have got a liquor licence if he had. Or maybe he would. She didn't really care. What mattered to her... all that mattered to her was that he loved her. Totally and utterly, and in a way she had never been loved before.

And Stanley Talbot had changed. Utterly and completely. That was because of love. He'd gone from being a criminal to a man who wanted to make amends for his past actions. Clearly anything was possible.

Hermione had said that the files would arrive by courier and would be beautifully wrapped gifts. It was too late for Elodie to get a courier but it wasn't too late to wrap a gift. And while Archer wasn't looking, she could add that gift to the pile of presents beneath the Christmas tree in his sitting room. He would never know it was from her. She could write the same note that Hermione had said had been written on the other gifts saying it was from Stanley. She could say she'd found it under one of the trees downstairs in the bar and had taken it up to the sitting room.

Or was that the wrong thing to do? Was that a lie? Should she just hand him the file and tell him the truth?

In the end, she decided on the latter, so as she and Archer were about to exchange one gift at midnight on Christmas Eve, she handed him the file which she had nevertheless wrapped beautifully.

'What's this?' he asked when he opened it and saw a thick, red file.

'It's one of the files from Stanley's office. One that the thief didn't steal.'

'It's got my name on it.' He seemed surprised. More than surprised. He looked shocked.

'Let me explain,' she said.

She wondered if he'd shout or get annoyed but he didn't. He sat and listened as she told him everything, including all about Hermione Dunmore and why his file wasn't with the ones that had been stolen.

'So you're telling me that Stanley kept files on everyone in the village and this is one of them? That you've had it in your bedroom but you haven't read one word? That you're giving it to me because this Hermione Dunmore is giving the files to everyone else?'

'Yes. But I think I would've given you this regardless of Hermione. Are you cross? Do you believe I haven't read it?'

He looked at the file and then at her.

'I'm not cross. At least not with you. And Stanley's no longer here so there's no point being cross with him. And yes. I do believe you. I wish you'd told me about it sooner but I can understand why you didn't.'

'Do you know what it might contain?'

'I have a good idea. Stanley wasn't a nice man, although from what Hermione told you, he changed. Completely changed, when he fell in love with her. I suppose the more important question is, do you want to know what it contains?'

Elodie looked at the file and then directly into Archer's eyes, her heart fit to burst with the love she saw there.

'I don't care what it contains. I love you Archer Rhodes. I trust you. You might've done things in your past you're not proud of. There might be things that Stanley thought he could blackmail you with. But the truth is, I don't care. You'll tell me what they are if you want to, when the time feels right. But if you'd rather not, I can live with that. What's in the past isn't important. It's what's in the future that counts.'

'I love you too. And I honestly don't know why he thought he could blackmail me. The things I've done aren't that bad. And I will tell you everything one day soon. But not today. Not Christmas Eve. Well, almost Christmas Day. Personally, I think we should burn this, but I'll happily let you read it first if you want to.'

'I don't. Nothing in that file could change the way I feel. Let's burn it.'

He smiled and pulled her close, kissing her so tenderly at first but then with such passion that the file and everything else was forgotten for some time.

They made love twice and cuddled for half an hour after. As they sat in front of the fire, Archer picked up the file, ready to toss the thing into the flames.

'Ready?' Archer said, smiling lovingly at her.

'Ready,' she replied mirroring that loving smile.

But as the file left his hand, she reached out and pushed it away from the flames, yelling, 'No, wait!'

'You've changed your mind?'

He looked a little crestfallen but she grabbed the file and handed it back to him, kissing him lightly on the nose.

'No. Well, yes. But not for the reason you think. Iris and I thought red meant bad – as in the devil kind of bad when we first saw the files, but her dad, Frank told us that Stanley had a colour code. Red meant wealth because red was his favourite colour.'

'That makes sense,' Archer said. 'And that's one of the things I was going to tell you. So I may as well tell you that now. I'm rich.'

'What?'

He nodded. 'A millionaire, as it happens, but at the moment, mainly on paper. Although it did mean I could buy the pub from Mum and Dad and pay for the refurbishment.' He laughed. 'And no, I didn't steal it in case you were wondering. I worked with a friend of mine, building houses for a while and when he wanted to start his own business I went in with him by investing my earnings in the company. He runs it from day to day and I leave him to it because I love running this pub. But he's recently negotiated a deal to sell that company and, as part-owner it means I'll be getting a pretty hefty pay out.'

'Wow! That is a surprise.'

'A good one, I hope.'

'Yes. And no.'

'No? Why no? The money won't change me. Although … I want to use some of it to see if I can reopen the search for my child. You'd be okay with that, wouldn't you?'

'Of course I would. And that wasn't what concerned me. I suddenly had a thought what might be in that file and why Stanley thought he could extort money from you, but maybe it wasn't what I was thinking. Maybe it was because he knew you were about to become rich, instead.'

'Instead of what?'

'Instead of the information I suddenly thought he might have in the file.'

'Which was ...?'

'Well, if all the things in your past aren't too terrible and he couldn't blackmail you to keep something quiet, maybe he had something that he thought you'd pay him *not* to keep quiet about.'

'Not to keep quiet? Sorry. You've lost me.'

'I may be wrong. Entirely wrong. But I think it's worth a look. What if Stanley either knew, or had an idea of, where your child might be? You'd have paid a lot for that information, wouldn't you? And maybe the reason the file is so thick is because he had to do a lot of digging to discover where that might be. Frank said Stanley had a knack of getting information about anyone and anything. I don't want to get your hopes up but I do think you should check.'

Archer didn't respond at first. He didn't do anything. He simply sat there looking at the file while the flames in the fire flickered and hissed and spat as if laughingly telling them how close they came to throwing away what Archer had been searching for all these years.

Archer swallowed as if something was stuck in his throat and then he took Elodie's hand in his.

'Let's open it together.'

Archer gave a strange sort of shriek when it quickly became clear that the file contained precisely what Elodie thought it might – all the details of Archer's long-lost child – a daughter. A daughter who was adopted by a family in Melbourne after her grandparents were killed in a car crash. A daughter who looked beautiful and healthy in the photos – all the photos Stanley had acquired from somewhere or other and that ranged in age from baby photos to the last photo taken at Elizabeth's nineteenth birthday party.

'Elizabeth. Her name is Elizabeth.' There were tears of joy mingled with sadness and disbelief in Archer's eyes.

'It's a beautiful name for a beautiful girl, Archer. And I don't think there can be any doubt that she's your daughter. She's the spitting image of you. Right down to the colour of her hair and eyes. And this may not be the time to mention it but it really is a small world. My sister lives in Melbourne. I've got a ticket to go out and visit and my parents are out there right now. You could come with me – or go on your own if you'd rather – and you can finally go and meet your daughter. But not until the New Year, sadly. Because all the airports are closed due to the snow.'

Archer looked her in the eye, a smile so wide it almost split his face in two.

'I'm not going anywhere without you, Elodie, so yes, I'll go with you, or you can come with me. Whatever. We'll go together. And I can wait until the New Year. I've waited for twenty-one years, I think I can wait a little longer. Especially with you by my side. I can face anything, do anything now that you are here with me. This is the best Christmas I've ever had. And to think, I nearly threw that file on the fire, but thanks to you, I've found my daughter.'

'Actually, I think we have to thank Stanley. And I never thought I'd be saying that.'

He laughed and carefully placing the file on the floor, far away from the fire, he pulled her into his arms. 'I love you with all my heart. Merry Christmas, Elodie, my darling.'

'I love you with all of my heart too. Merry Christmas, Archer.'

They were just about to kiss when Elodie's phone rang.

'Let me guess,' Archer said. 'That's Iris calling to wish us a Merry Christmas.'

Elodie laughed as she answered the phone. 'And probably to find out what time we'll be at Clementine Cottage for Christmas breakfast.'

'Merry Christmas!' Iris yelled down the phone. 'And yes, that's why I was calling.'

'Merry Christmas, Iris. And wish Bentley, Merry Christmas too.'

'We'll be late,' Archer said. 'Merry Christmas, Iris, and goodbye for now.'

'Oh. Okay. I can take a hint.' Iris laughed. 'See you later! Have fun.'

'Very late,' Archer said as Elodie rang off and he took the phone from her. 'Because I want to spend most of Christmas morning in bed with the best present any man could wish for. And believe me, I did wish for you. Every year until this one I wished for happiness for my child and that's always been my wish in my bottle. This year I made two wishes. Happiness for my child and I wished you would love me as much as I loved you. I want to spend the morning in bed with the love of my life. And that is you, Elodie Abbott, in case you had any doubts.'

'No doubts. Not one. And I wished you would love me as much as I had fallen in love with you! We both got our wishes, Archer. I knew this year would be special and the good news is, I think it's only going to get better from hereon. Now weren't you about to kiss me?'

'I was and I am. Several times, in fact.'

Coming soon

Please see my website for details.
www.emilyharvale.com

A Note from Emily

A little piece of my heart goes into every one of my books and when I send them on their way, I really hope they bring a smile to someone's face. If this book made you smile, or gave you a few pleasant hours of relaxation, I'd love you to tell your friends. And if you have a minute or two to post a review (just a few words will do) that would be lovely too. A kind review makes such a difference to any author's day. Huge thanks to those of you who do so, and for your wonderful comments and support on social media. Thank you.
A writer's life can be lonely at times. Sharing a virtual cup of coffee or a glass of wine, or exchanging a few friendly words via my website Open House, or on Facebook, Twitter or Instagram is so much fun.

I mentioned my newsletter earlier. It's absolutely free, your email address is safe and won't be shared and I won't bombard you, I promise. You can enter competitions and enjoy some giveaways. In addition to that, there's my author page on Facebook. There's also my lovely, Facebook group and now my wonderful, Emily's Open House (both mentioned earlier) where you'll meet me, and other fans, and get access to my book news, sometimes early extracts from my books and lots more besides. You'll find all my contact links on my website and in the Contact section in this book. Hope to chat with you soon.

I can't wait to bring you more stories that I hope will capture your heart, mind and imagination, allowing you to escape into a world of romance in some enticingly beautiful settings.

Also by Emily Harvale

The Golf Widows' Club
Sailing Solo
Carole Singer's Christmas
Christmas Wishes
A Slippery Slope
The Perfect Christmas Plan
Be Mine
It Takes Two
Bells and Bows on Mistletoe Row

Lizzie Marshall series:
Highland Fling – book 1
Lizzie Marshall's Wedding – book 2

Goldebury Bay series:
Ninety Days of Summer – book 1
Ninety Steps to Summerhill – book 2
Ninety Days to Christmas – book 3

Hideaway Down series:
A Christmas Hideaway – book 1
Catch A Falling Star – book 2
Walking on Sunshine – book 3
Dancing in the Rain – book 4

Hall's Cross series
Deck the Halls – book 1
The Starlight Ball – book 2

Michaelmas Bay series
Christmas Secrets in Snowflake Cove – book 1
Blame it on the Moonlight – book 2

Lily Pond Lane series

The Cottage on Lily Pond Lane – four-part serial
Part One – New beginnings
Part Two – Summer secrets
Part Three – Autumn leaves
Part Four – Trick or treat
Christmas on Lily Pond Lane
Return to Lily Pond Lane
A Wedding on Lily Pond Lane
Secret Wishes and Summer Kisses on Lily Pond Lane

Wyntersleap series

Christmas at Wynter House – Book 1
New Beginnings at Wynter House – Book 2
A Wedding at Wynter House – Book 3
Love is in the Air – spin off

Merriment Bay series

Coming Home to Merriment Bay – Book 1
(four-part serial)
Part One – A Reunion
Part Two – Sparks Fly
Part Three – Christmas
Part Four – Starry Skies
Chasing Moonbeams in Merriment Bay – Book 2
Wedding Bells in Merriment Bay – Book 3

Seahorse Harbour series

Summer at my Sister's – book 1
Christmas at Aunt Elsie's – book 2
Just for Christmas – book 3
Tasty Treats at Seahorse Bites Café – book 4
Dreams and Schemes at The Seahorse Inn – book 5
Weddings and Reunions in Seahorse Harbour – book 6

To see a complete list of my books, or to sign up for my newsletter, go to
www.emilyharvale.com/books

If you really love my books and want to be the first to see some sneak peeks, play book related games and connect with Emily and other fans, you can ask to become a Harvale Heart and gain a virtual key to Emily's Open House.
www.emilyharvale.com/MembersClub

There's also an exclusive Facebook group for fans of my books.
www.emilyharvale.com/FacebookGroup

Or scan the QR code below to see all my books on Amazon.

Stay in touch with

Emily Harvale

If you want to be the first to hear Emily's news, find out about book releases, see covers and maybe chat with other fans, there are a few options for you:

Visit: www.emilyharvale.com

and subscribe to Emily's newsletter via the 'sign me up' box. Or, if you really love Emily's books, apply to join Emily's Open House here:

www.emilyharvale.com/MembersClub

Or ask to join Emily's exclusive Facebook Group here:

www.emilyharvale.com/FacebookGroup

Alternatively, just come and say 'Hello' on social media:

 @EmilyHarvaleWriter

 @EmilyHarvale

 @EmilyHarvale

Printed in Great Britain
by Amazon